PRAISE FOR **squish!**

"Even the mildest young boy will see something of himself in Squish. *Super Amoeba* is an energetic, good-hearted escapade, one that young readers will enjoy."
—*The New York Times*

★"The hilarious misadventures of a hapless young everylad who happens to be an amoeba. If ever a new series deserved to go viral, this one does."
—*Kirkus Reviews*, Starred

"The Holms strike a breezy, goofy tone right out of the gate."
—*Publishers Weekly*

"A perfect mix of writing that is simple enough for early readers but still remarkably snarky, clever, and entertaining. . . . Kids themselves will soak up the humor, tidbits of science instruction, and adventure."
—*The Bulletin of the Center for Children's Books*

"A new graphic novel series that will have readers everywhere clapping their pseudopods in glee. There's some real science worked in here too and even directions for a kid-friendly experiment."
—*Bookends* (*Booklist* blog)

Read ALL the SQUISH books!

#1   SQUISH: Super Amoeba

#2   SQUISH: Brave New Pond

#3   SQUISH: The Power of the Parasite

squish
THE POWER OF THE PARASITE

BY JENNIFER L. HOLM & MATTHEW HOLM

RANDOM HOUSE NEW YORK

This is a work of fiction. Names, characters, places, and incidents either are the product of the authors' imagination or are used fictitiously. Any resemblance to actual persons, living or dead, events, or locales is entirely coincidental.

 Published in the United States by
Random House Children's Books,
a division of Random House, Inc., New York.
Random House and the colophon are
registered trademarks of Random House, Inc.

Visit us on the Web! randomhouse.com/kids
Educators and librarians, for a variety of teaching tools,
visit us at randomhouse.com/teachers

Library of Congress Cataloging-in-Publication Data
Holm, Jennifer L.
The power of the Parasite /
by Jennifer L. Holm and Matthew Holm. — 1st ed.
p. cm. — (Squish ; #3)
Summary: At swim camp, Squish's new friend Basil helps him avoid learning to swim with pranks that sometimes go too far, but the comic book exploits of Squish's idol, "Super Amoeba," help him deal with Basil and conquer his fear.
ISBN 978-0-375-84391-4 (trade pbk.) —
ISBN 978-0-375-93785-9 (lib. bdg.)
1. Graphic novels. [1. Graphic novels. 2. Amoeba—Fiction.
3. Camps—Fiction. 4. Practical jokes—Fiction.
5. Swimming—Fiction. 6. Superheroes—Fiction.]
I. Holm, Matthew. II. Title.
PZ7.7.H65Pow 2012 741.5'973—dc23 2011024120

MANUFACTURED IN MALAYSIA 10 9 8 7 6 5 4 3 2 1
First Edition

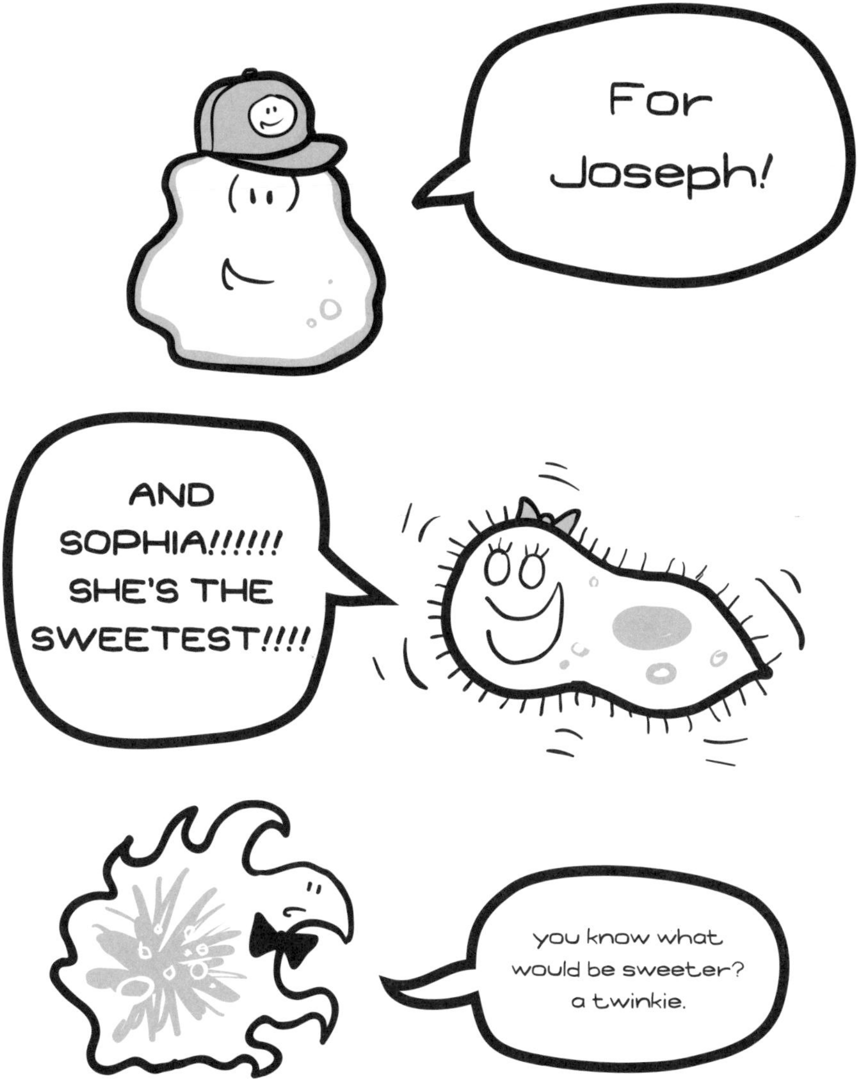
For Joseph!
AND SOPHIA!!!!!! SHE'S THE SWEETEST!!!!
you know what would be sweeter? a twinkie.

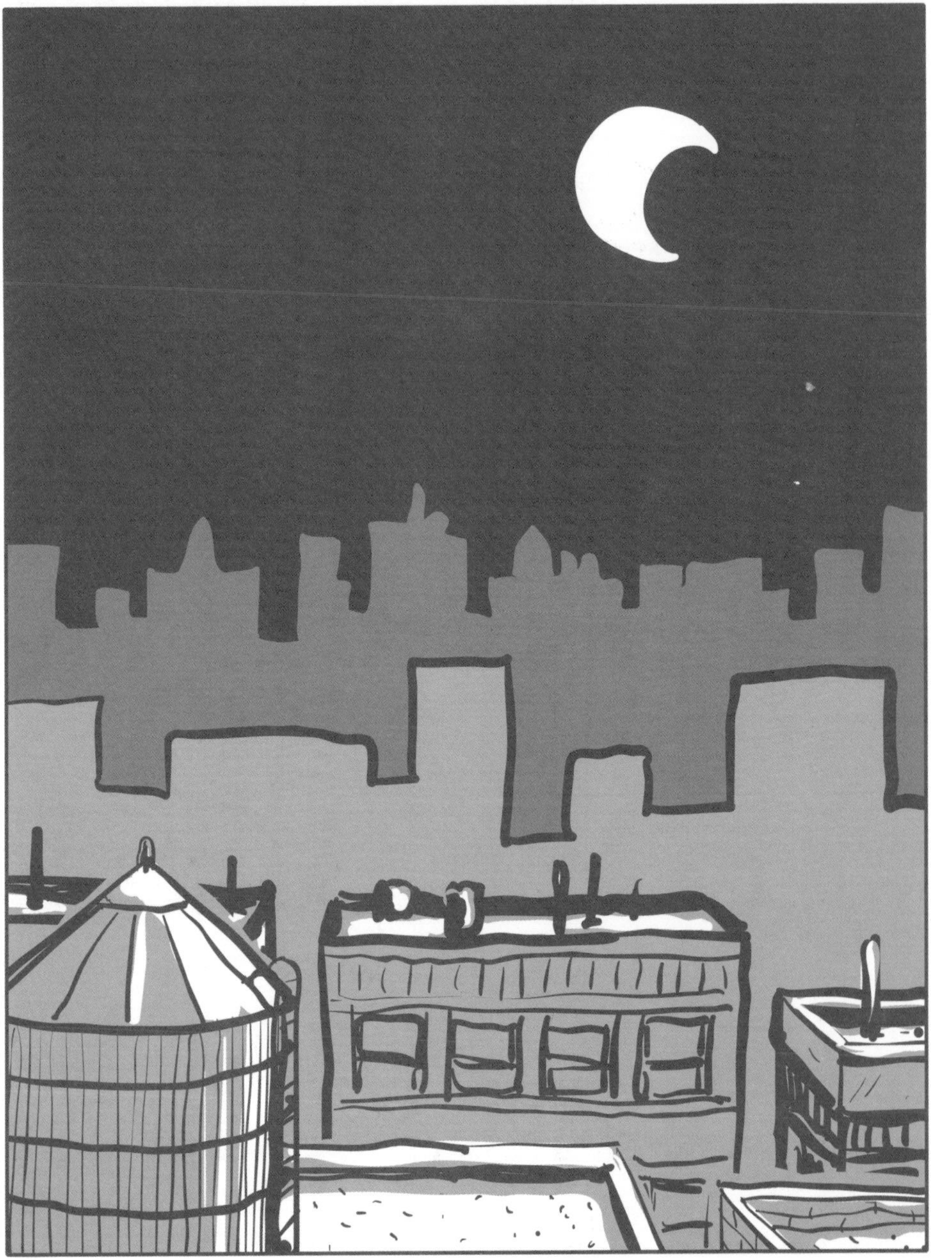

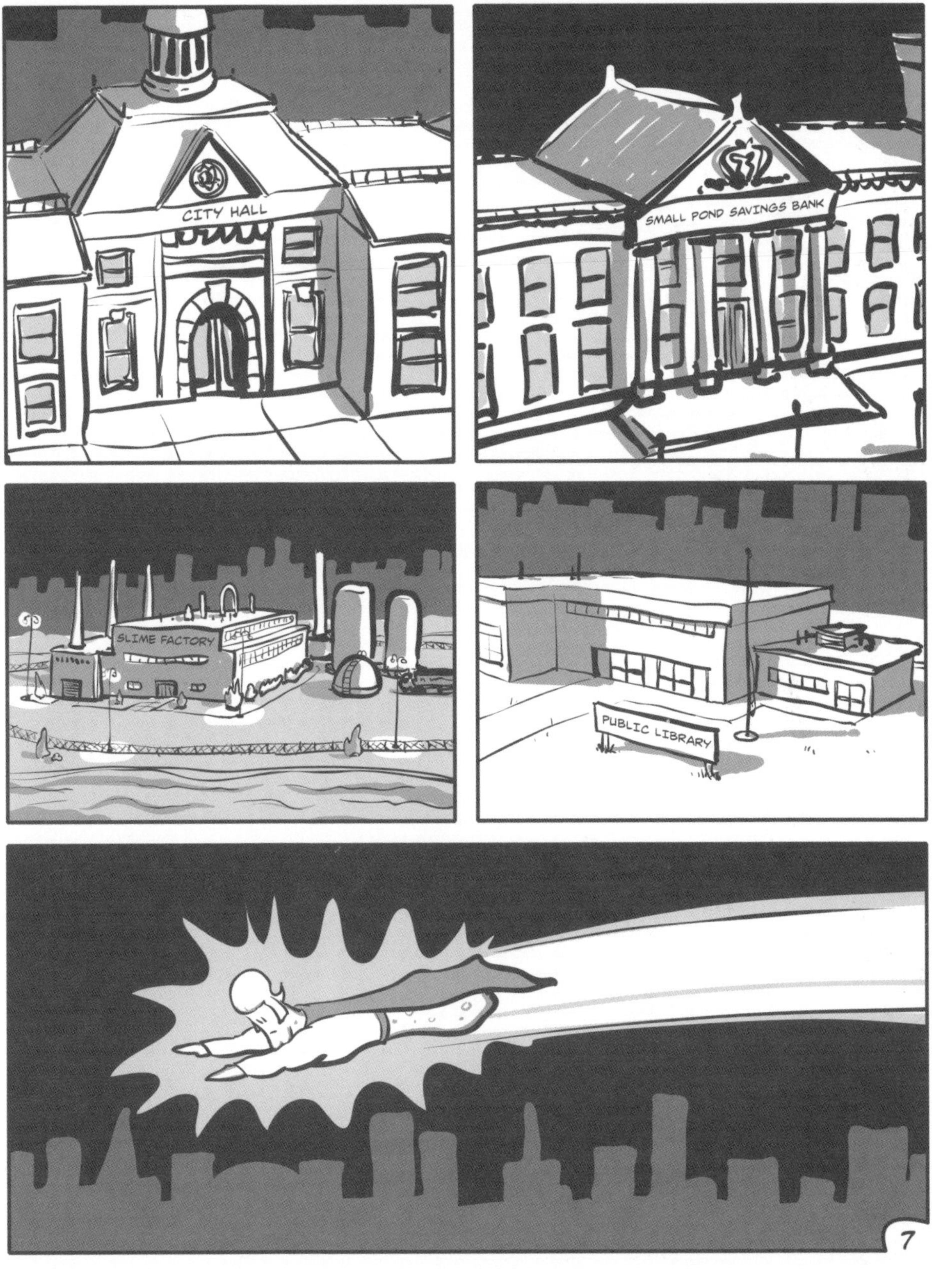
CITY HALL
SMALL POND SAVINGS BANK
SLIME FACTORY
PUBLIC LIBRARY

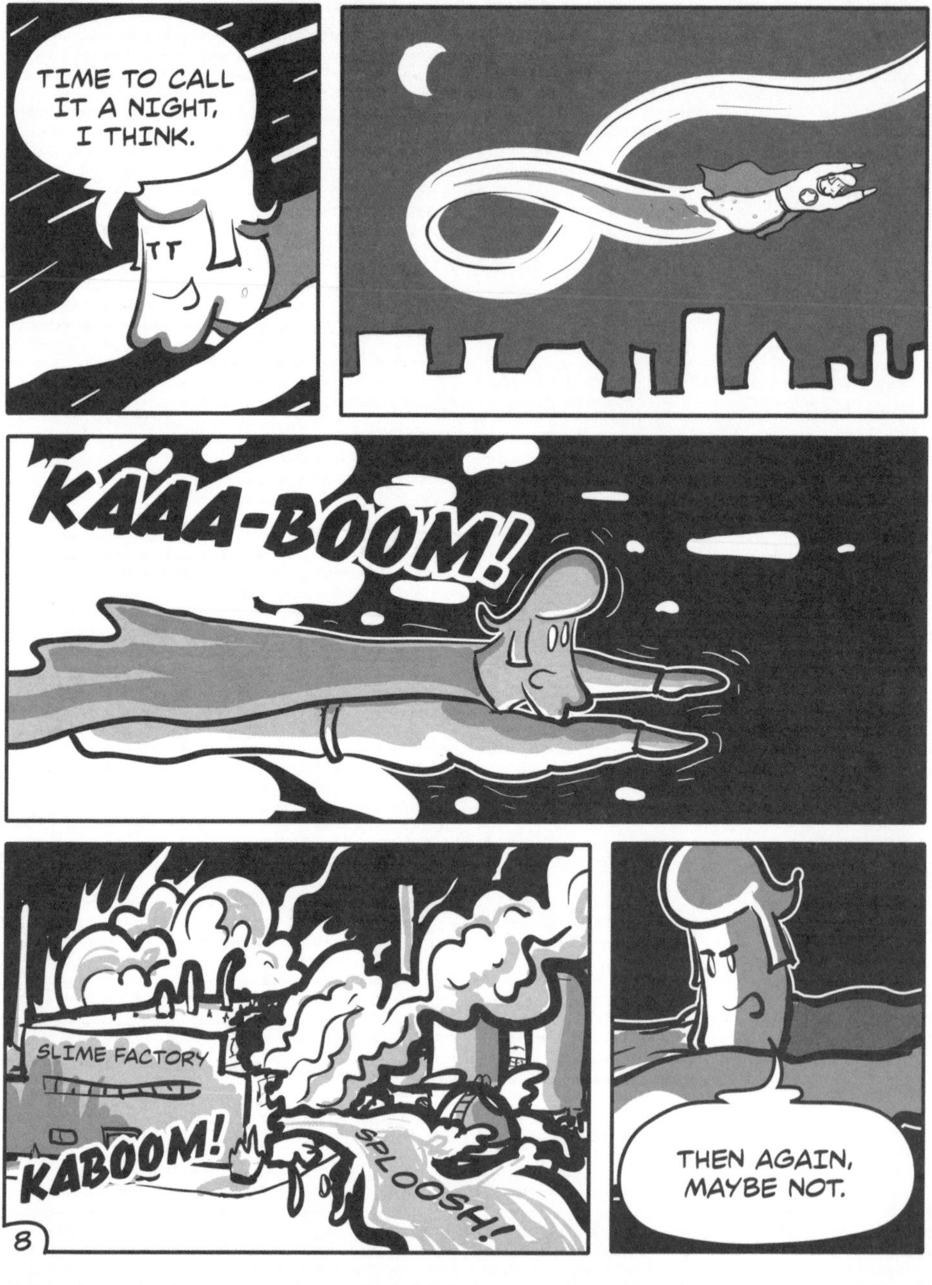
TIME TO CALL IT A NIGHT, I THINK.
KAAA-BOOM!
SLIME FACTORY
KABOOM!
SPLOOSH!
THEN AGAIN, MAYBE NOT.

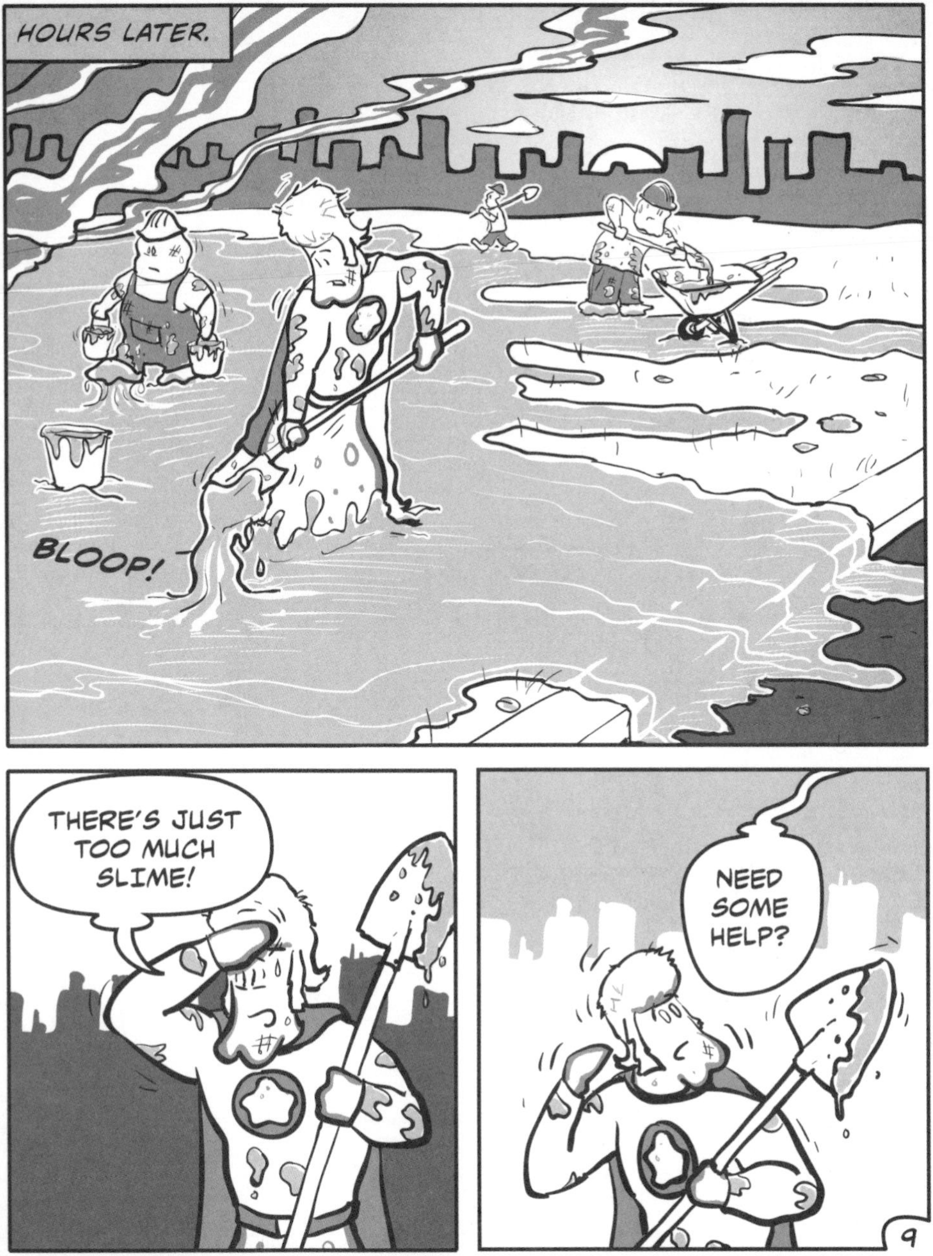
HOURS LATER.
BLOOP!
THERE'S JUST TOO MUCH SLIME!
NEED SOME HELP?

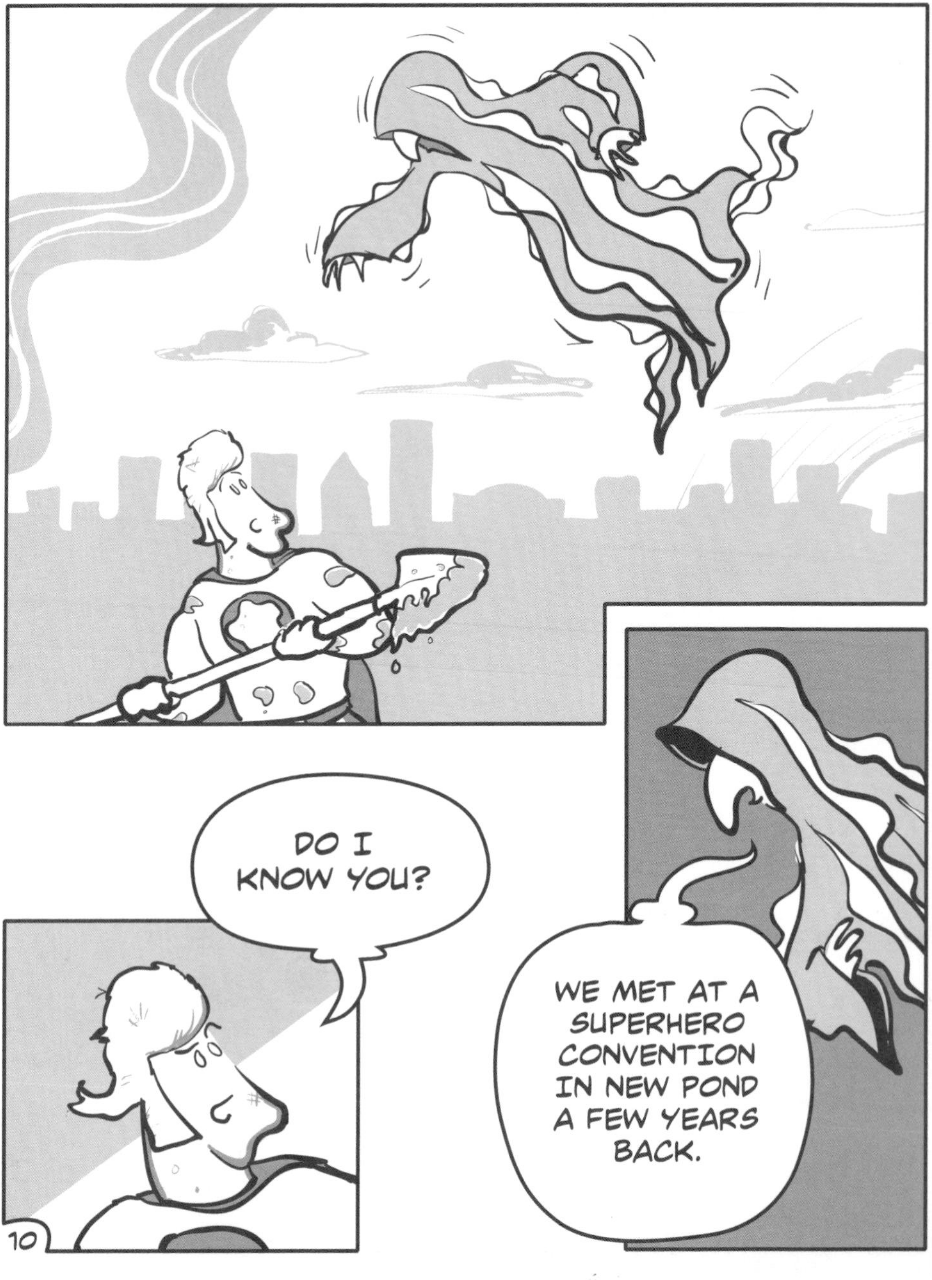
DO I KNOW YOU?
WE MET AT A SUPERHERO CONVENTION IN NEW POND A FEW YEARS BACK.

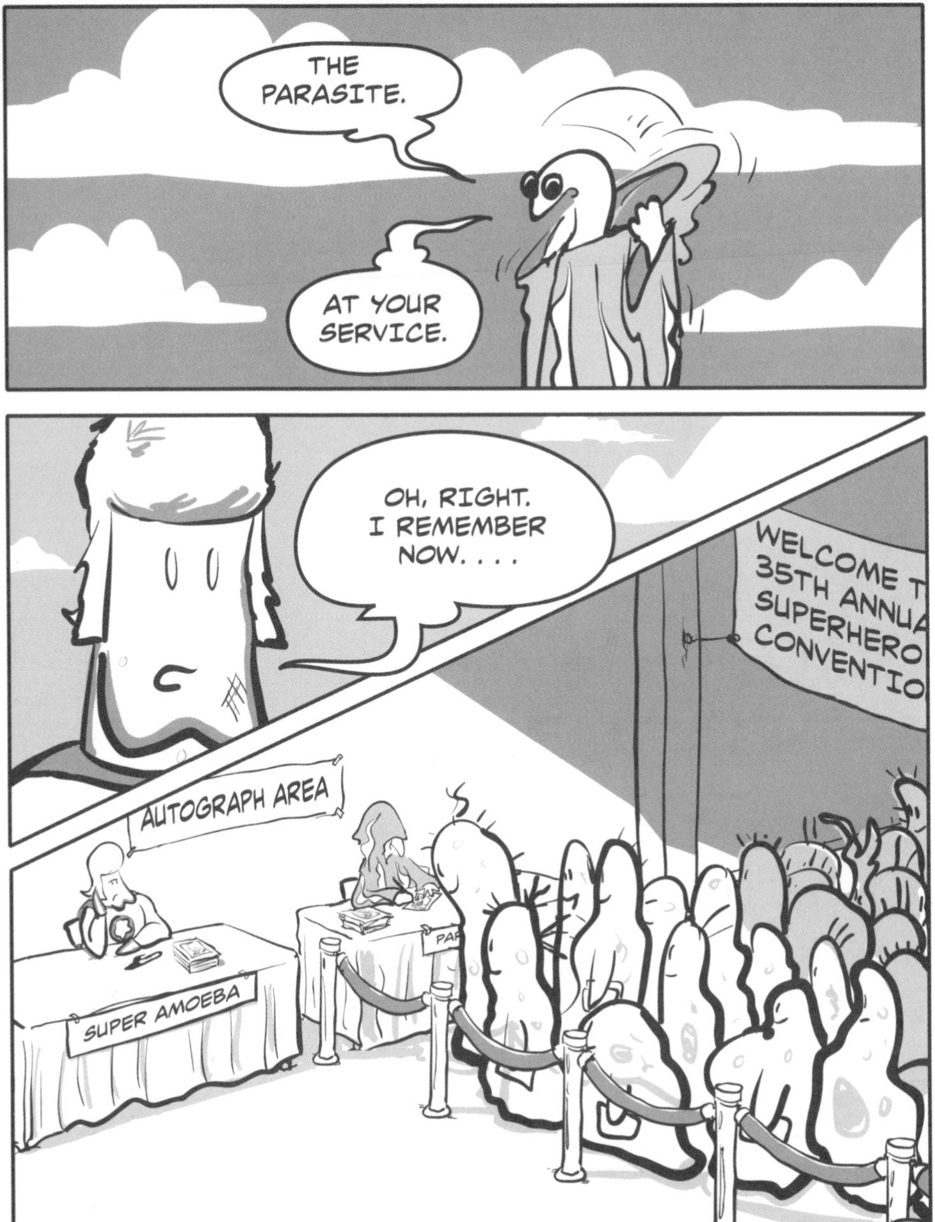
THE PARASITE.
AT YOUR SERVICE.
OH, RIGHT. I REMEMBER NOW. . . .
WELCOME T
35TH ANNUA
SUPERHERO
CONVENTIO
AUTOGRAPH AREA
SUPER AMOEBA

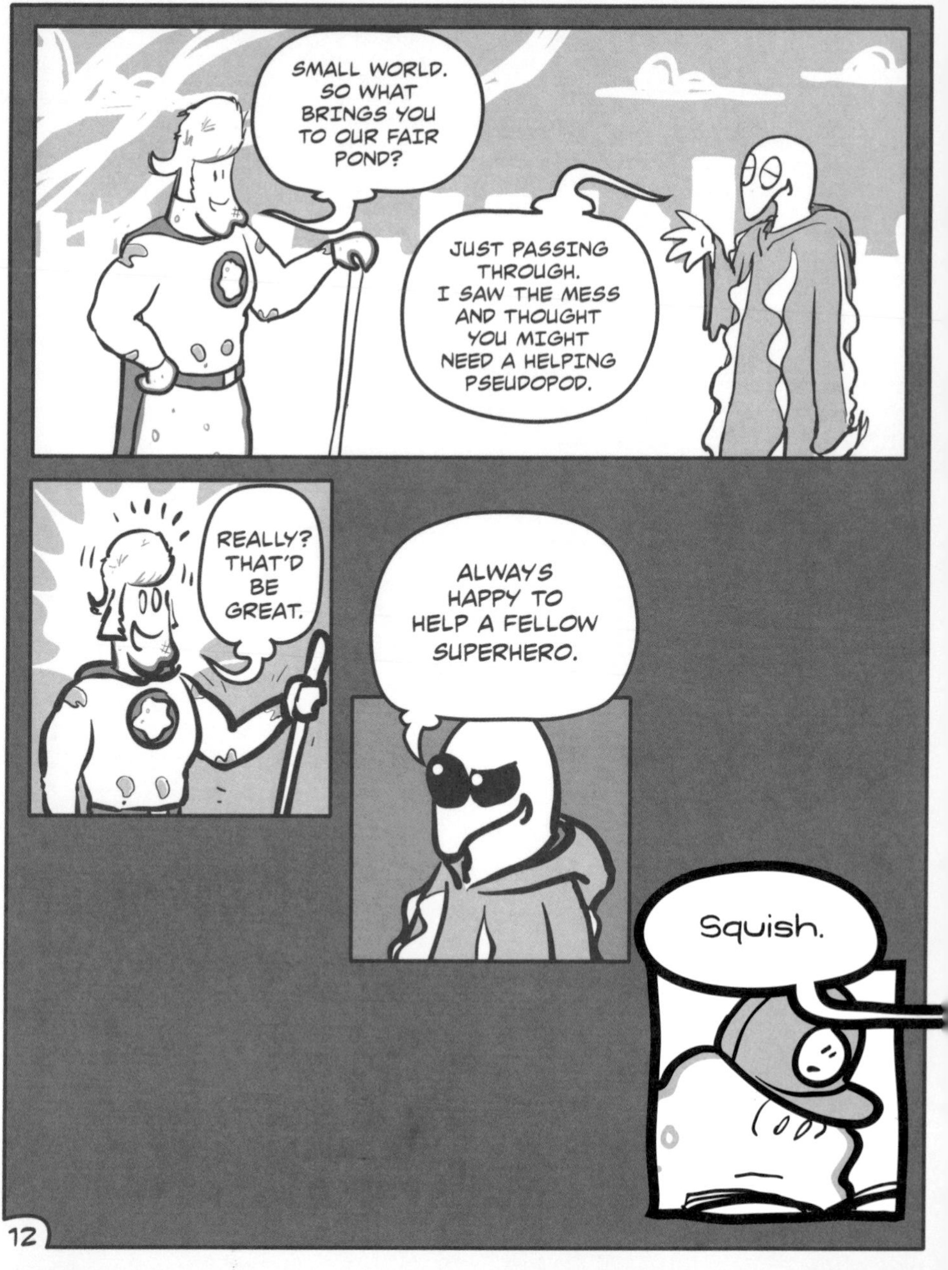
SMALL WORLD. SO WHAT BRINGS YOU TO OUR FAIR POND?
JUST PASSING THROUGH. I SAW THE MESS AND THOUGHT YOU MIGHT NEED A HELPING PSEUDOPOD.
REALLY? THAT'D BE GREAT.
ALWAYS HAPPY TO HELP A FELLOW SUPERHERO.
Squish.

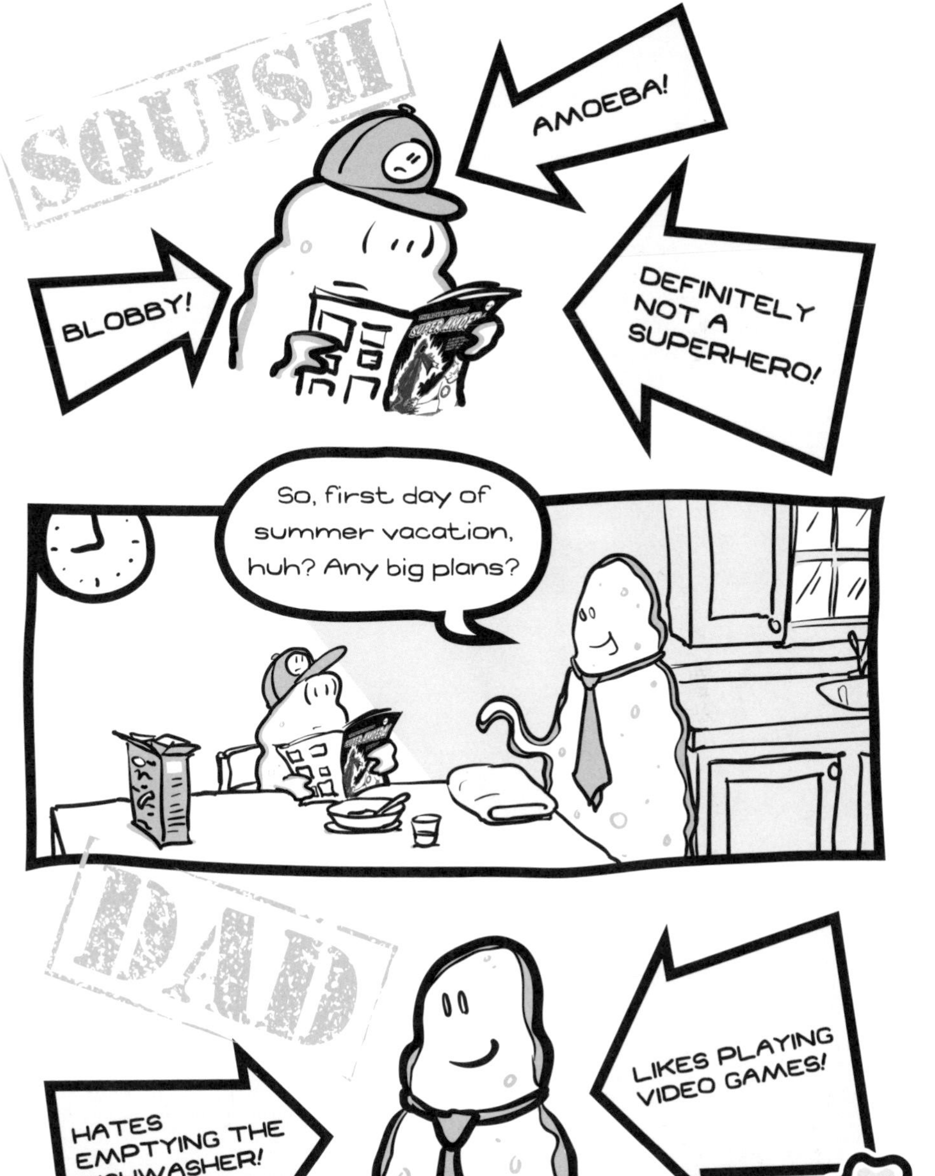
SQUISH
AMOEBA!
BLOBBY!
DEFINITELY NOT A SUPERHERO!
So, first day of summer vacation, huh? Any big plans?
DAD
LIKES PLAYING VIDEO GAMES!
HATES EMPTYING THE DISHWASHER!

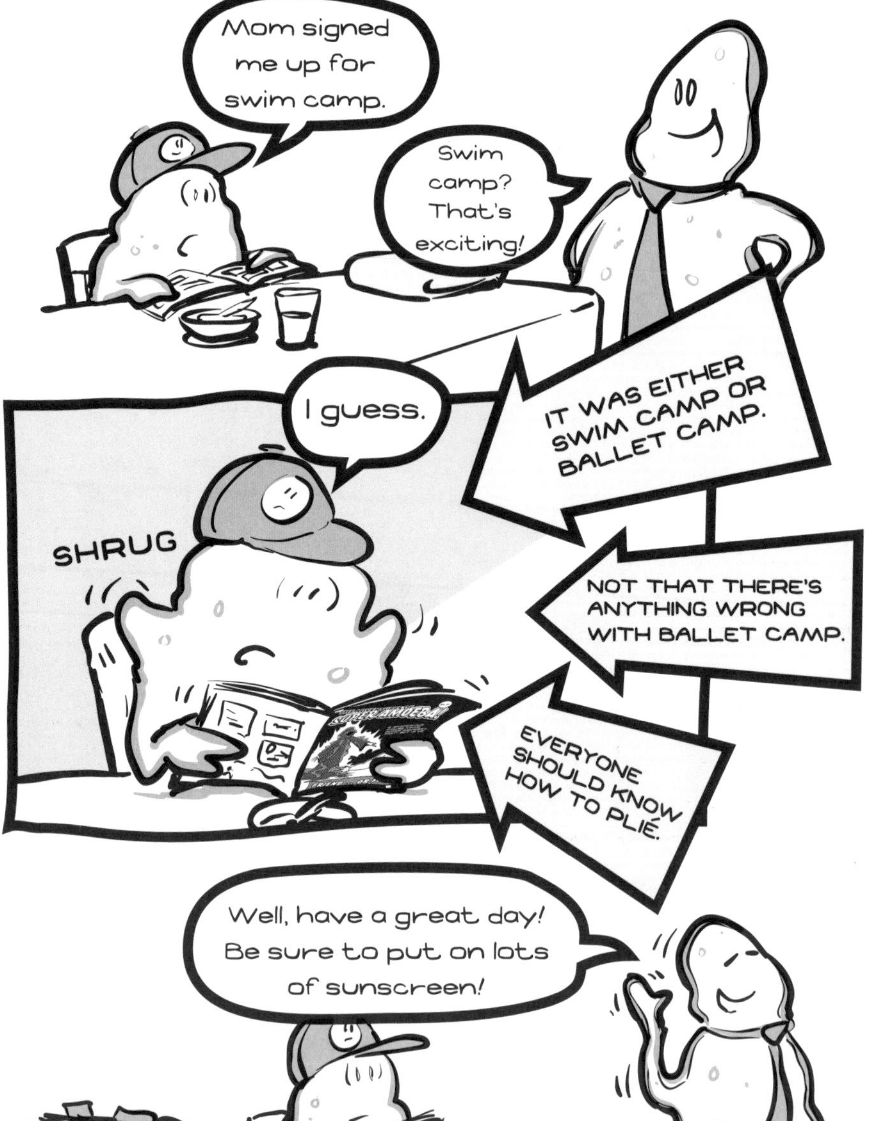
Mom signed me up for swim camp.
Swim camp? That's exciting!
I guess.
SHRUG
IT WAS EITHER SWIM CAMP OR BALLET CAMP.
NOT THAT THERE'S ANYTHING WRONG WITH BALLET CAMP.
EVERYONE SHOULD KNOW HOW TO PLIÉ.
Well, have a great day! Be sure to put on lots of sunscreen!

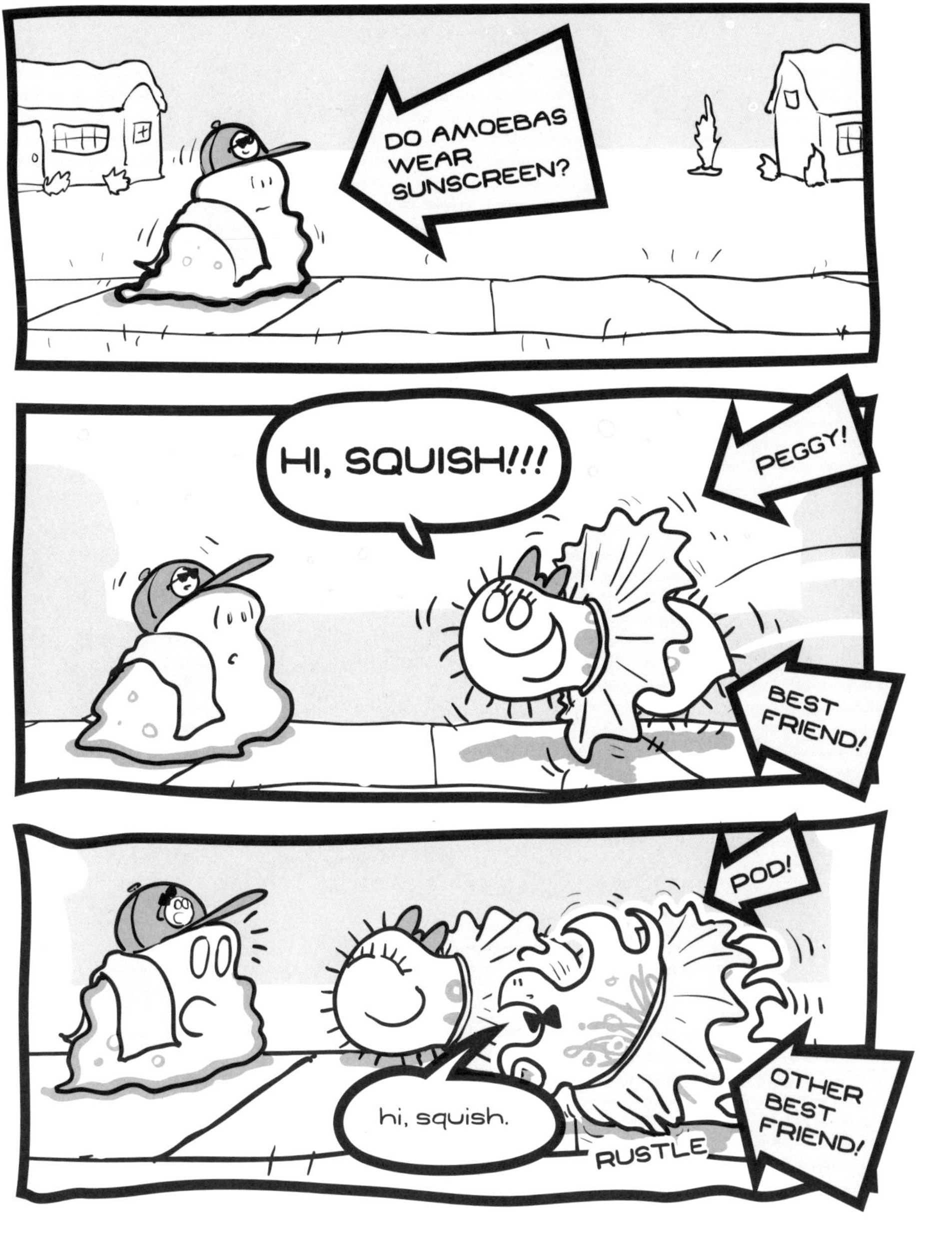
DO AMOEBAS WEAR SUNSCREEN?
HI, SQUISH!!!
PEGGY!
BEST FRIEND!
POD!
hi, squish.
RUSTLE
OTHER BEST FRIEND!

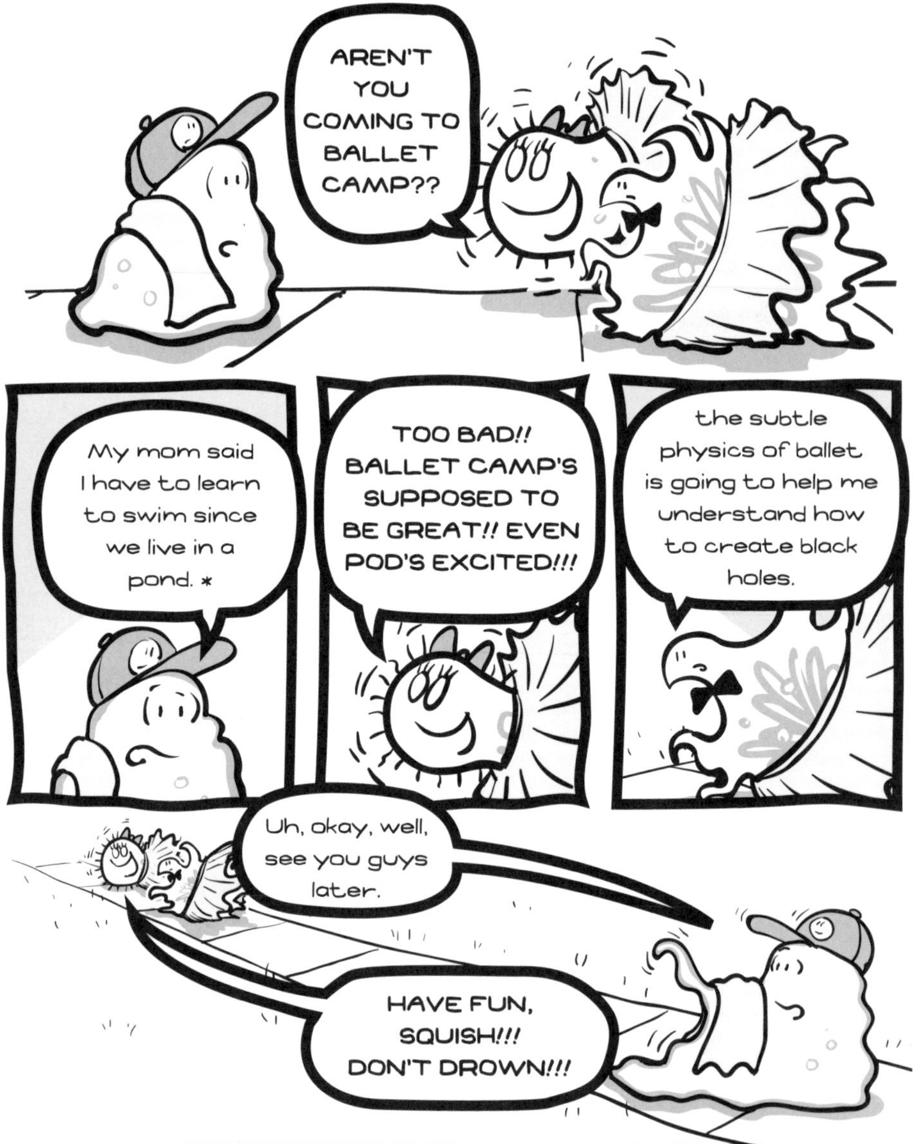
AREN'T YOU COMING TO BALLET CAMP??
My mom said I have to learn to swim since we live in a pond. *
TOO BAD!! BALLET CAMP'S SUPPOSED TO BE GREAT!! EVEN POD'S EXCITED!!!
the subtle physics of ballet is going to help me understand how to create black holes.
Uh, okay, well, see you guys later.
HAVE FUN, SQUISH!!! DON'T DROWN!!!

* SCIENTIFIC FACT: AMOEBAS LIVE IN PONDS. THAT'S ENOUGH SCIENCE FOR TODAY.

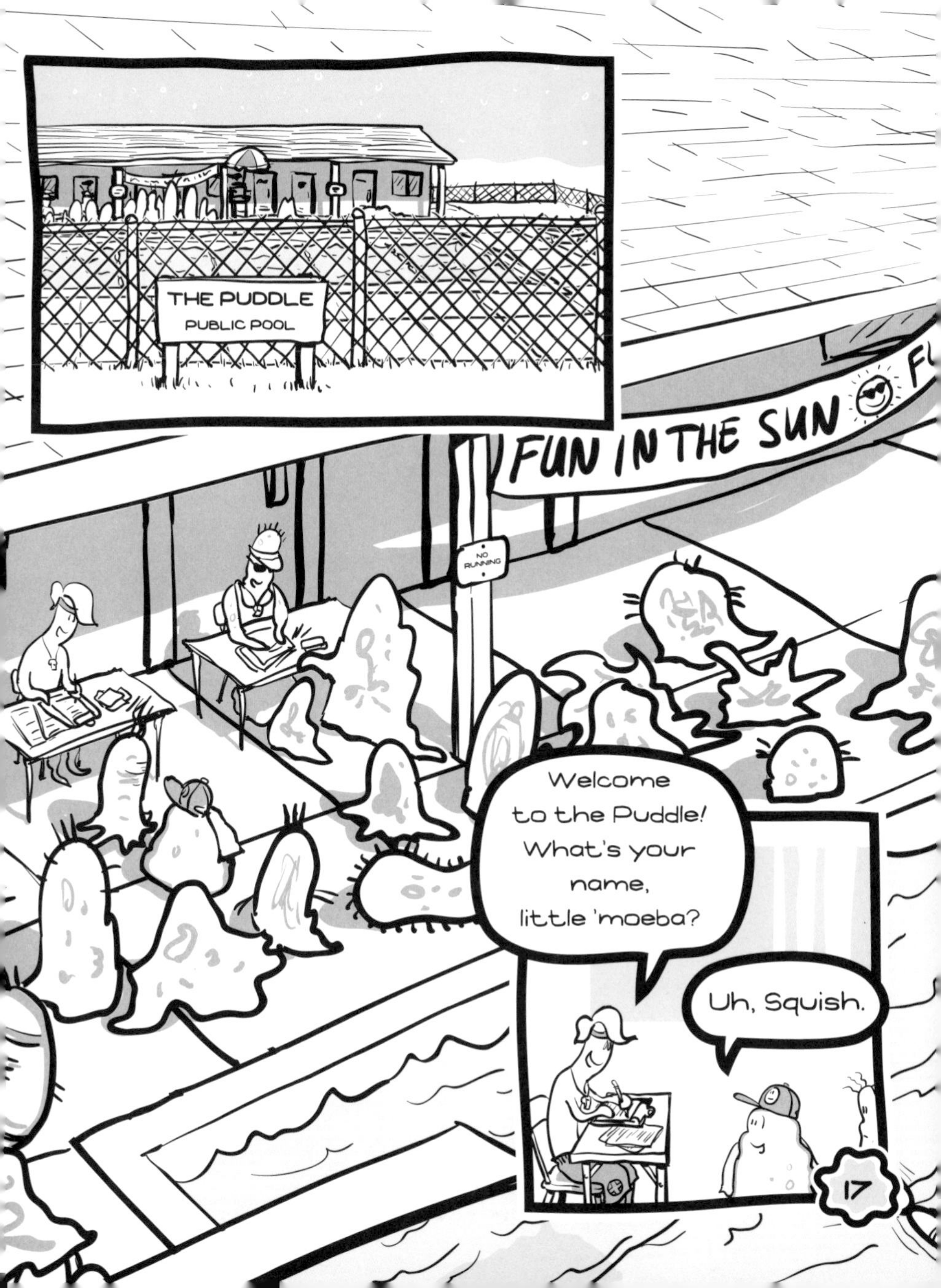
THE PUDDLE
PUBLIC POOL
FUN IN THE SUN
NO RUNNING
Welcome to the Puddle! What's your name, little 'moeba?
Uh, Squish.
17

Here you go, Squash. Go hang up your towel and grab some grass.

MY NAME IS

SQUASH

Sigh.

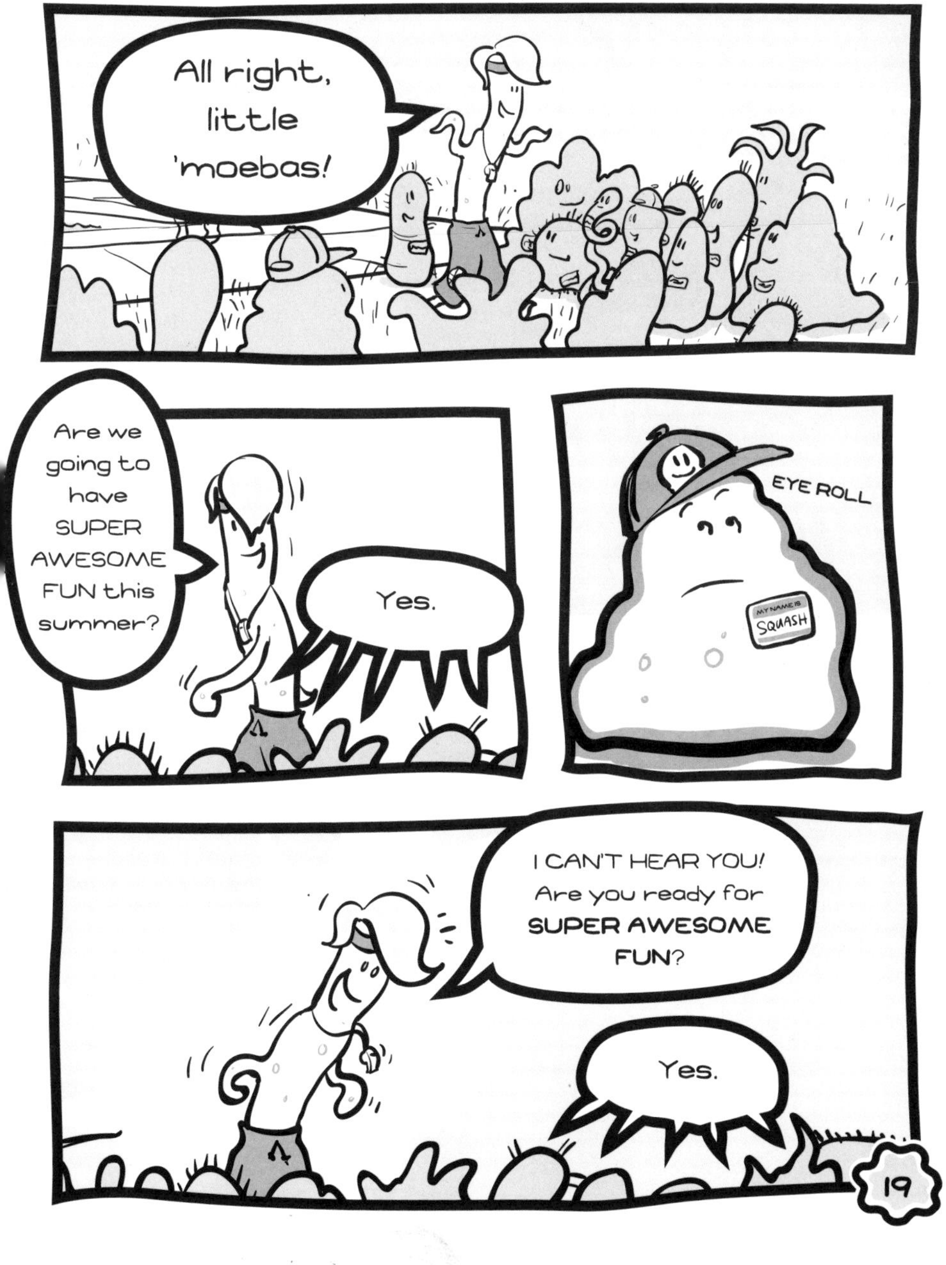
All right, little 'moebas!
Are we going to have SUPER AWESOME FUN this summer?
Yes.
EYE ROLL
MY NAME IS SQUASH
I CAN'T HEAR YOU! Are you ready for SUPER AWESOME FUN?
Yes.

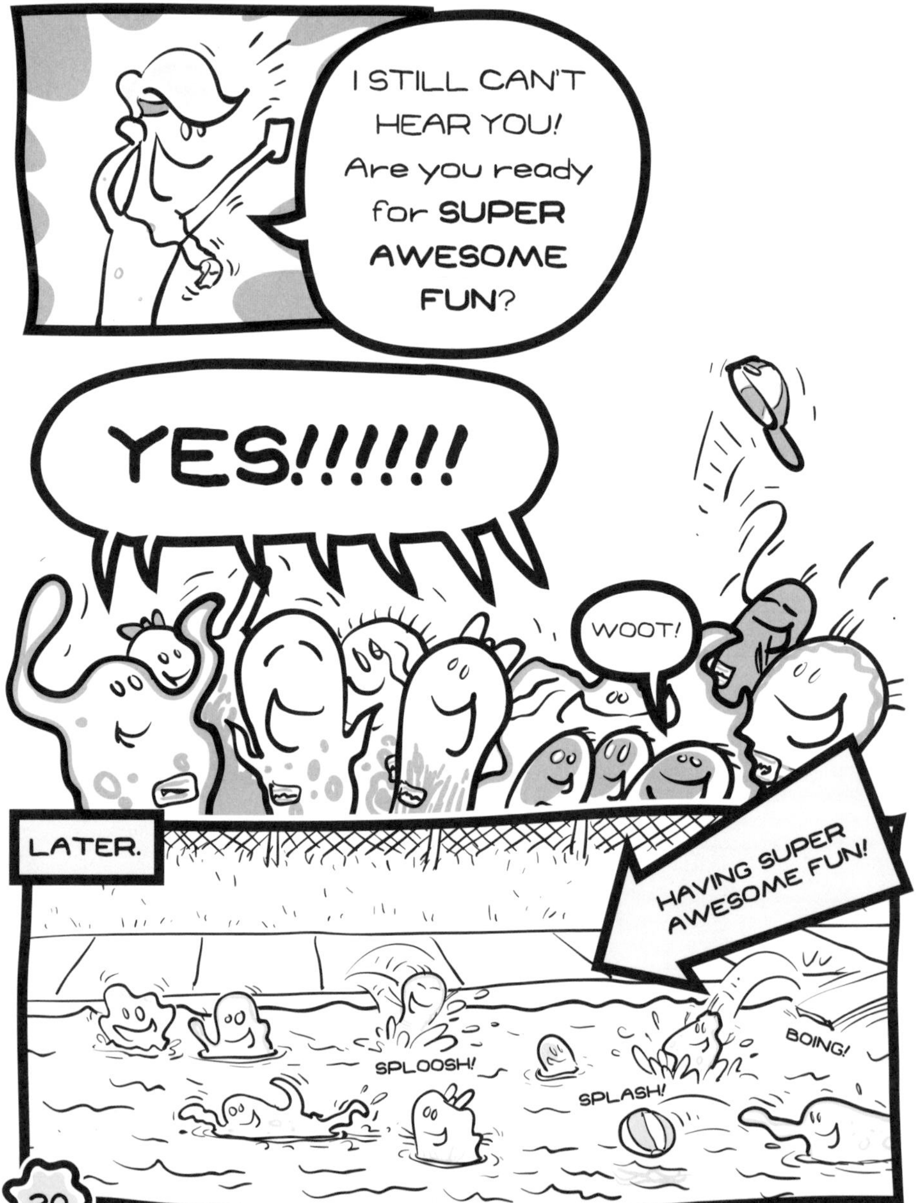
I STILL CAN'T HEAR YOU! Are you ready for SUPER AWESOME FUN?
YES!!!!!!!
WOOT!
LATER.
HAVING SUPER AWESOME FUN!
SPLOOSH!
SPLASH!
BOING!

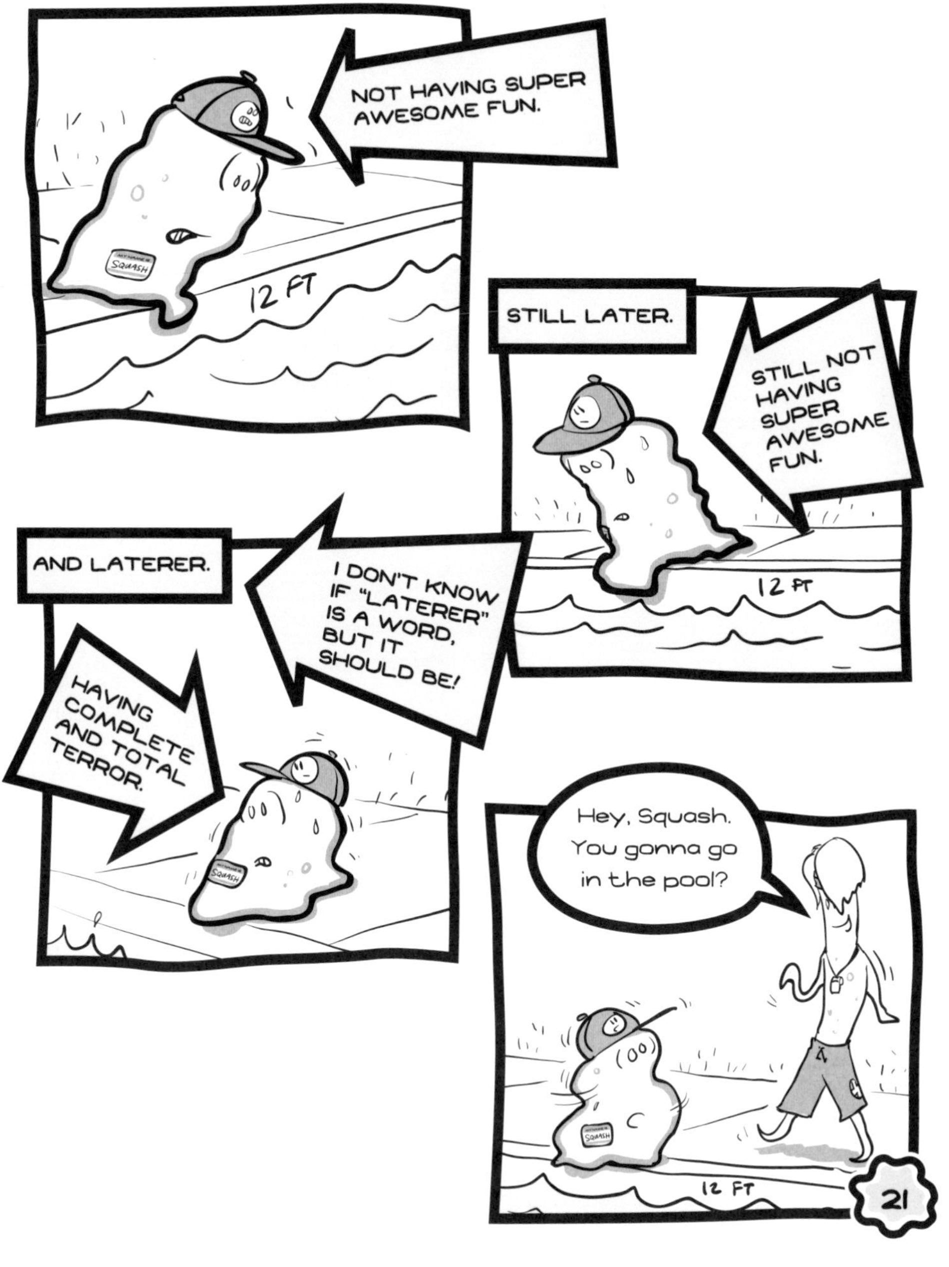
NOT HAVING SUPER AWESOME FUN.
SQUASH
12 FT
STILL LATER.
STILL NOT HAVING SUPER AWESOME FUN.
12 FT
AND LATERER.
I DON'T KNOW IF "LATERER" IS A WORD, BUT IT SHOULD BE!
HAVING COMPLETE AND TOTAL TERROR.
SQUASH
Hey, Squash. You gonna go in the pool?
SQUASH
12 FT

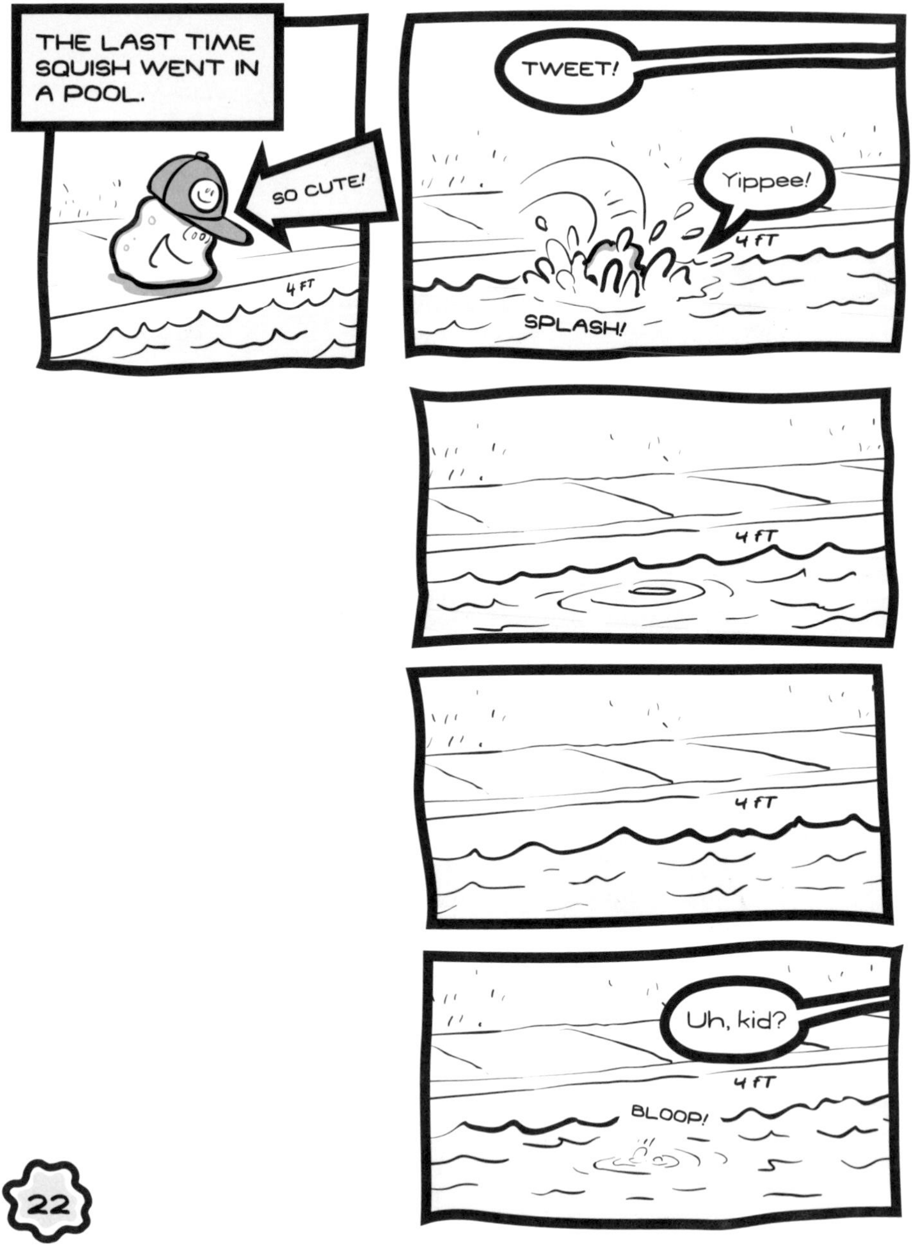
THE LAST TIME SQUISH WENT IN A POOL.
SO CUTE!
4 FT
TWEET!
Yippee!
4 FT
SPLASH!
4 FT
4 FT
Uh, kid?
4 FT
BLOOP!

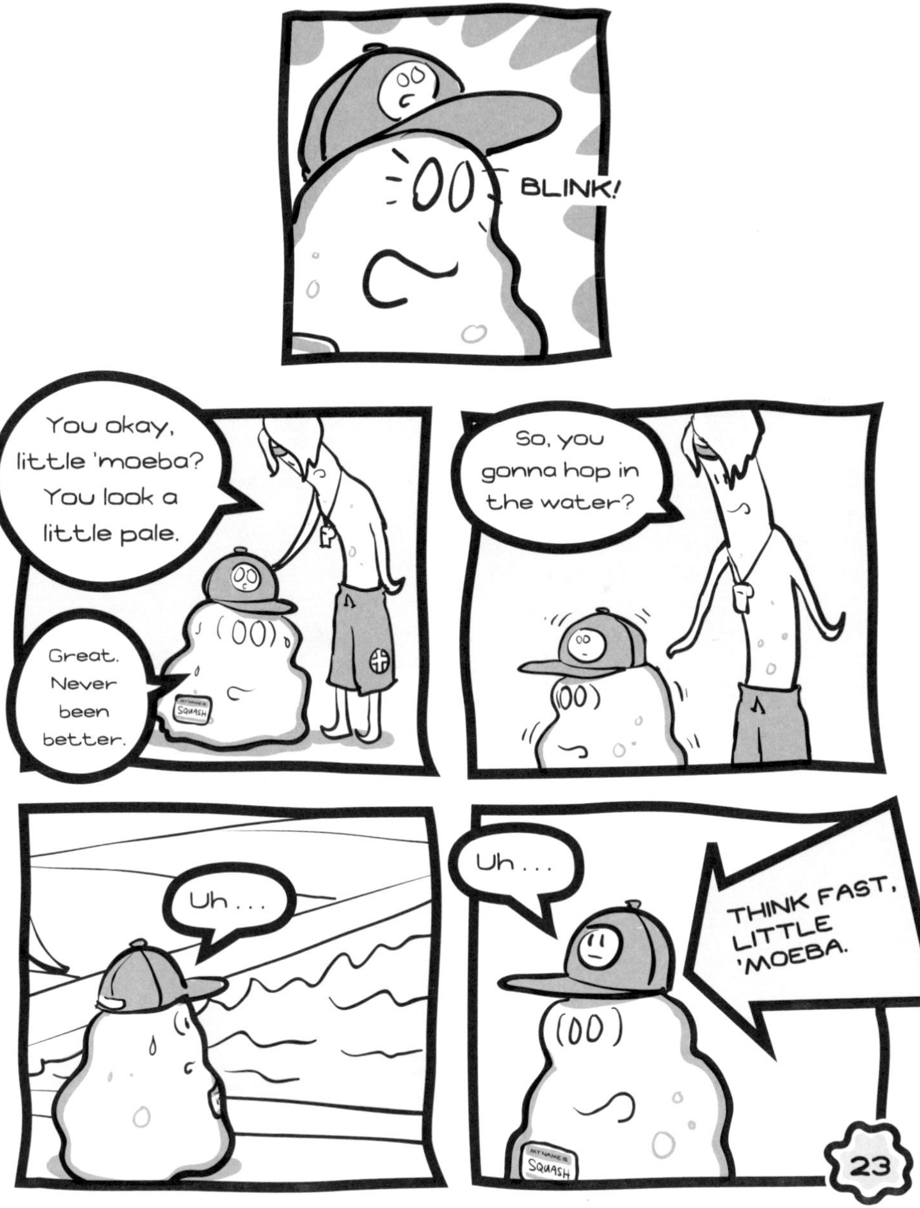
BLINK!
You okay, little 'moeba? You look a little pale.
Great. Never been better.
So, you gonna hop in the water?
Uh . . .
Uh . . .
THINK FAST, LITTLE 'MOEBA.
MY NAME IS SQUASH

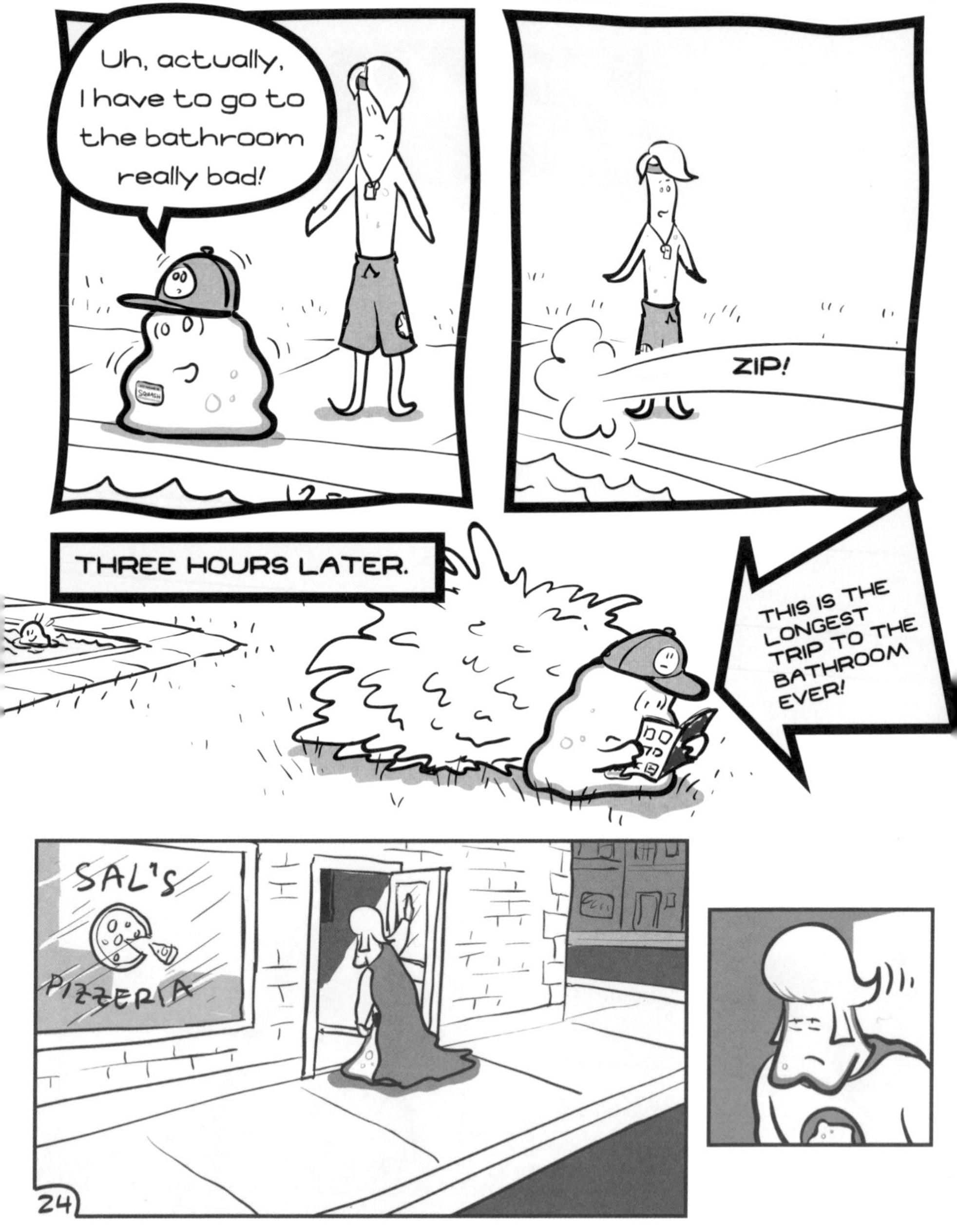
Uh, actually, I have to go to the bathroom really bad!
SQUASH
ZIP!
THREE HOURS LATER.
THIS IS THE LONGEST TRIP TO THE BATHROOM EVER!
SAL'S PIZZERIA

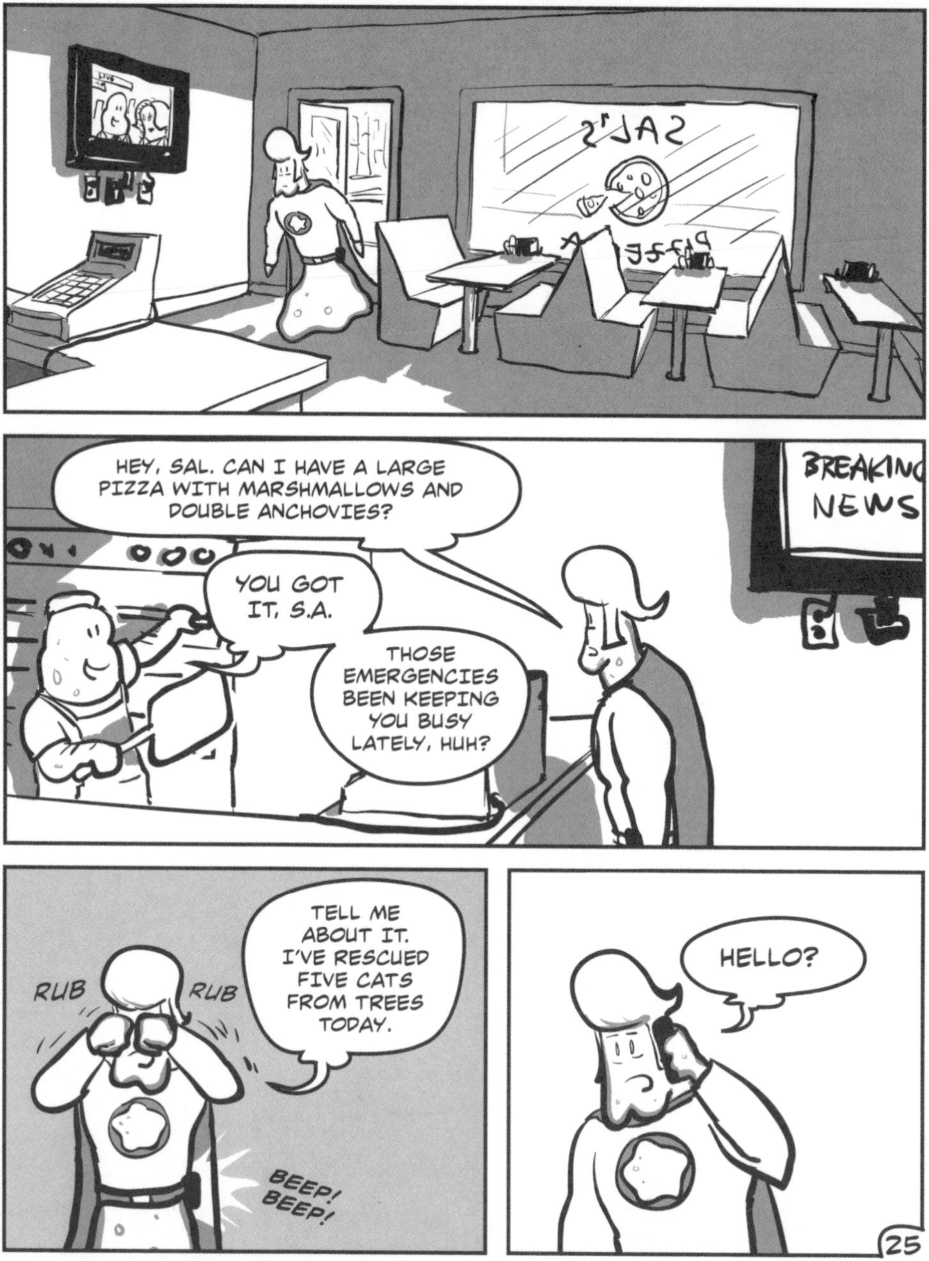
SAL'S
PIZZA
BREAKING NEWS
HEY, SAL. CAN I HAVE A LARGE PIZZA WITH MARSHMALLOWS AND DOUBLE ANCHOVIES?
YOU GOT IT, S.A.
THOSE EMERGENCIES BEEN KEEPING YOU BUSY LATELY, HUH?
RUB RUB
TELL ME ABOUT IT. I'VE RESCUED FIVE CATS FROM TREES TODAY.
BEEP! BEEP!
HELLO?

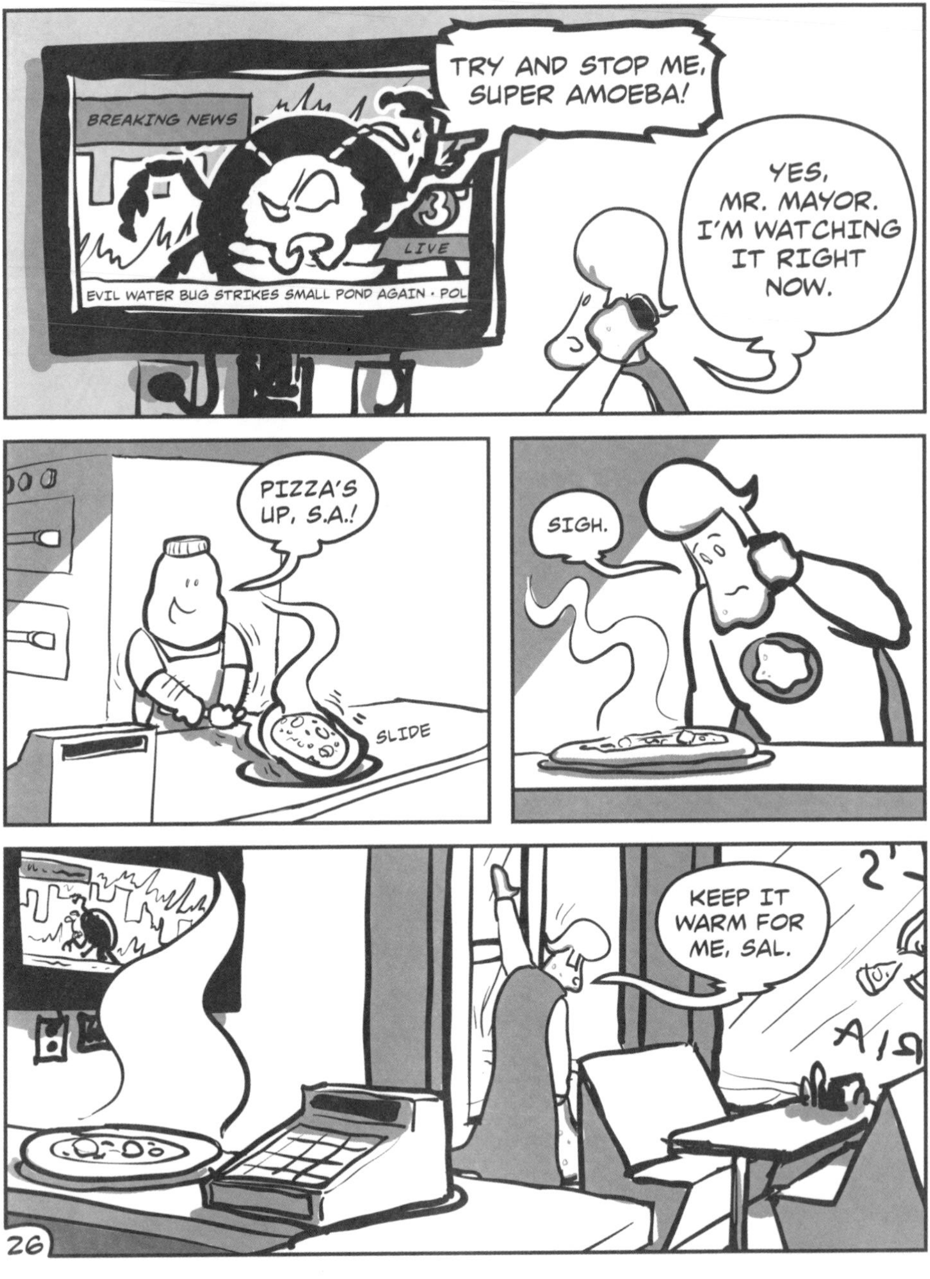
BREAKING NEWS
LIVE
EVIL WATER BUG STRIKES SMALL POND AGAIN • POL
TRY AND STOP ME, SUPER AMOEBA!
YES, MR. MAYOR. I'M WATCHING IT RIGHT NOW.
PIZZA'S UP, S.A.!
SLIDE
SIGH.
KEEP IT WARM FOR ME, SAL.

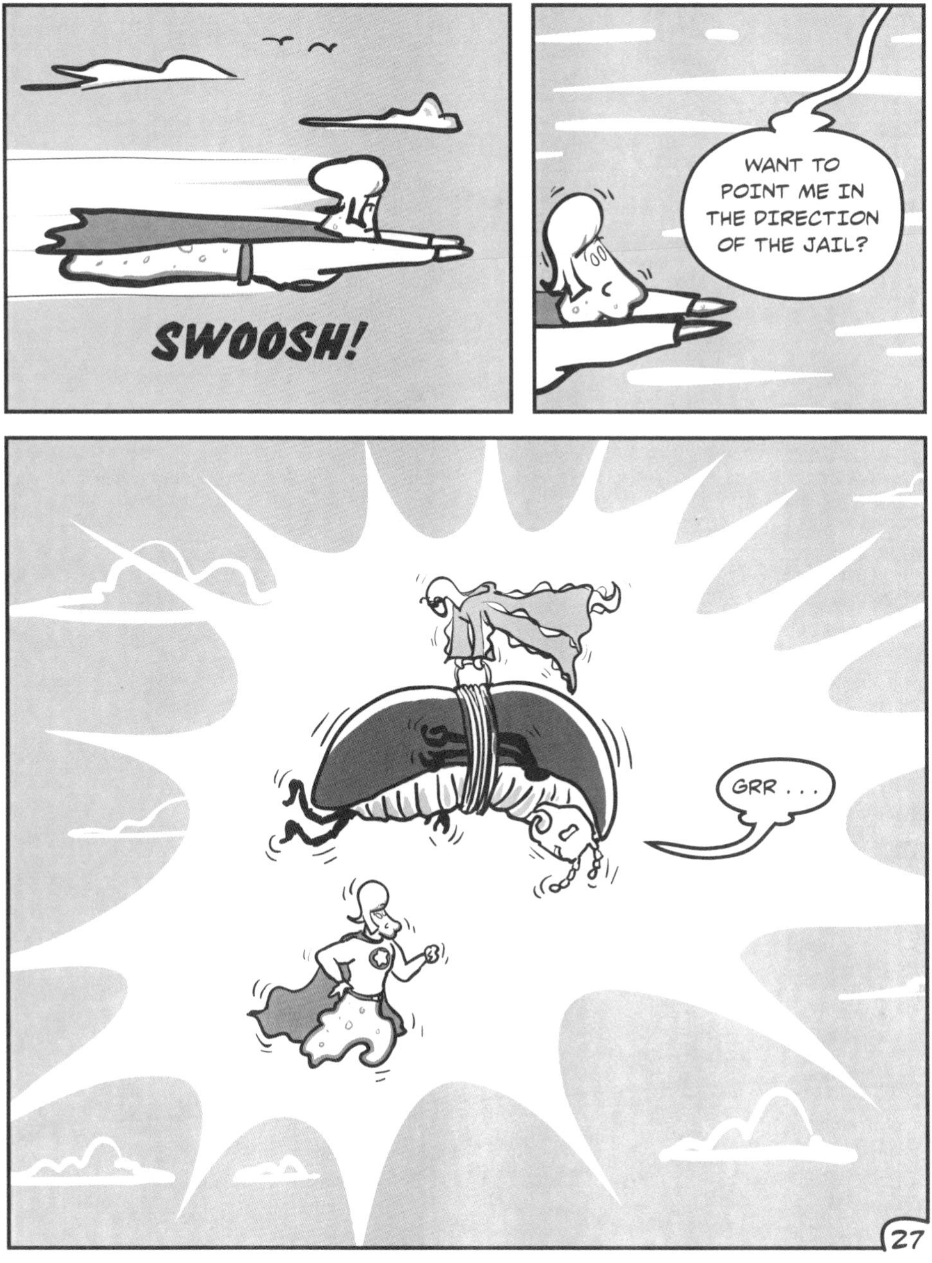
SWOOSH!
WANT TO POINT ME IN THE DIRECTION OF THE JAIL?
GRR . . .

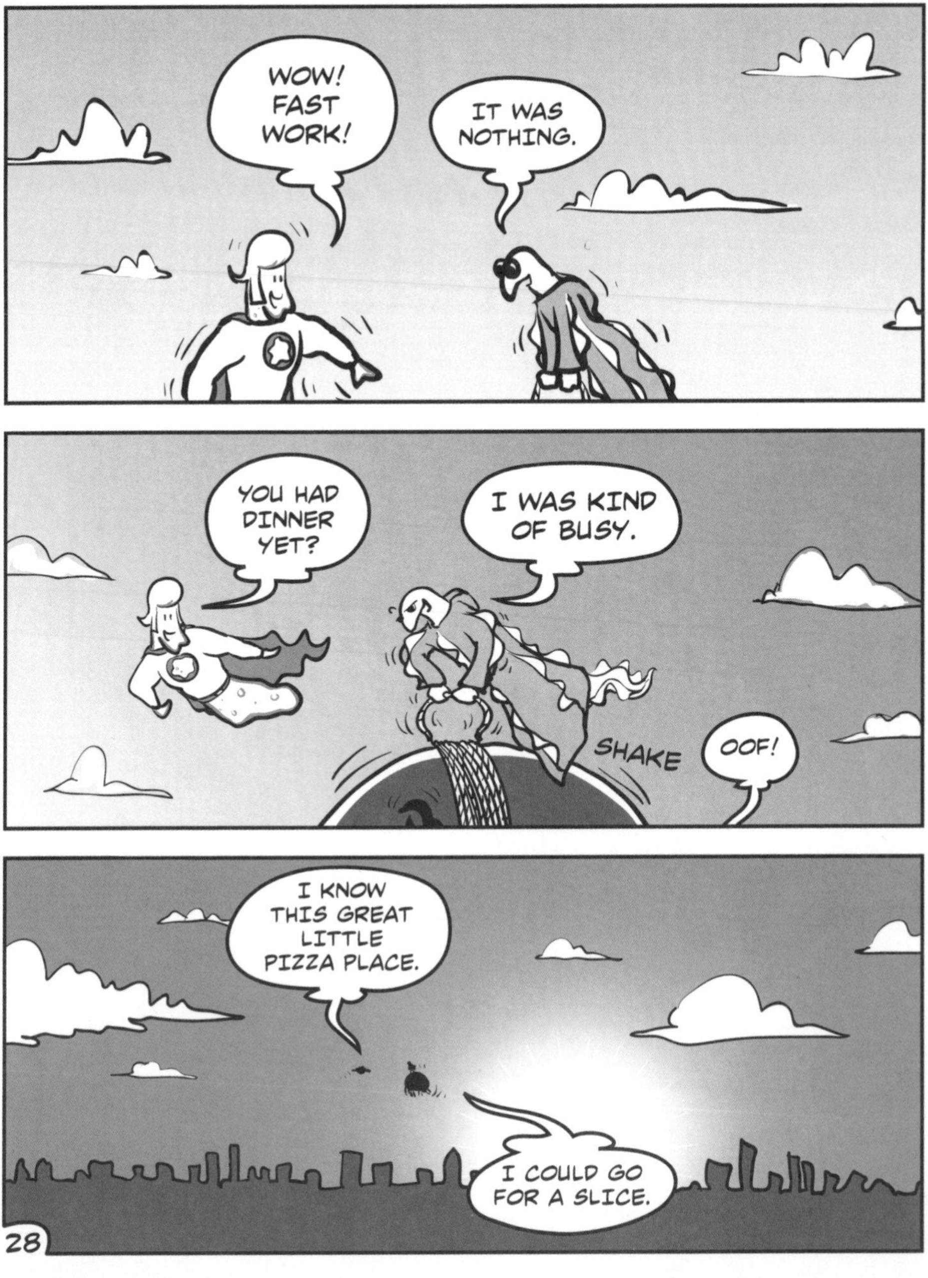
WOW! FAST WORK!
IT WAS NOTHING.
YOU HAD DINNER YET?
I WAS KIND OF BUSY.
SHAKE
OOF!
I KNOW THIS GREAT LITTLE PIZZA PLACE.
I COULD GO FOR A SLICE.

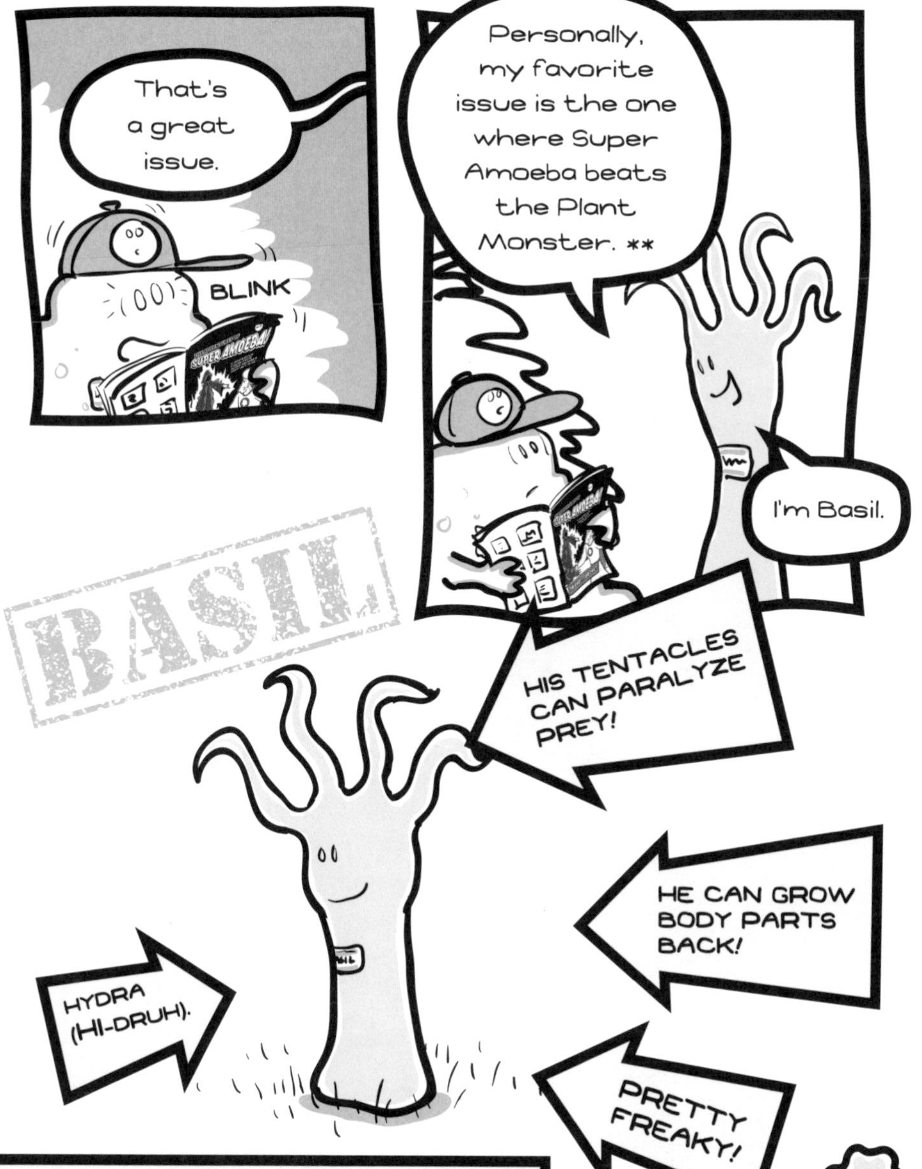
That's a great issue.
BLINK
Personally, my favorite issue is the one where Super Amoeba beats the Plant Monster. **
I'm Basil.
BASIL
HIS TENTACLES CAN PARALYZE PREY!
HE CAN GROW BODY PARTS BACK!
HYDRA (HI-DRUH).
PRETTY FREAKY!

** READ SQUISH #1: SUPER AMOEBA!

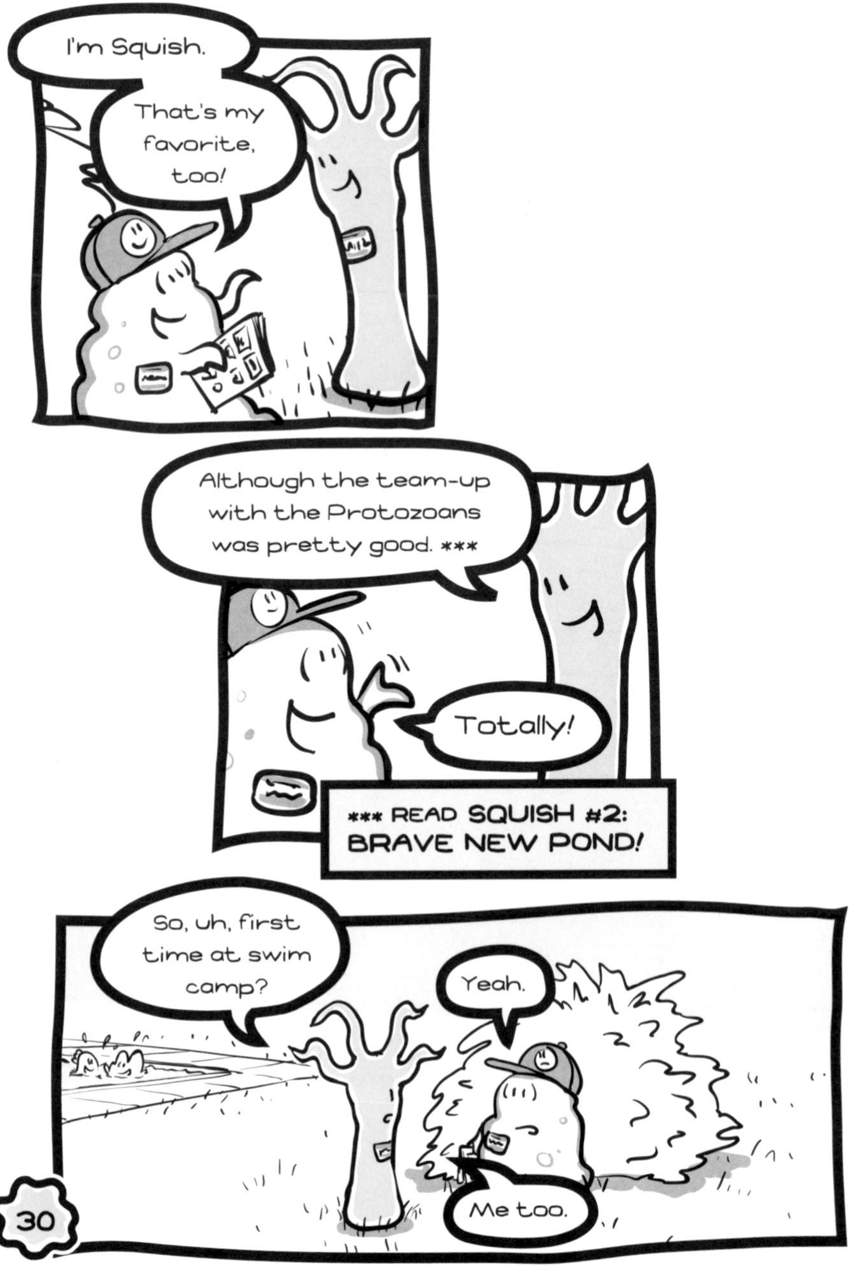

I'm Squish.
That's my favorite, too!
Although the team-up with the Protozoans was pretty good. ***
Totally!
*** READ SQUISH #2: BRAVE NEW POND!
So, uh, first time at swim camp?
Yeah.
Me too.

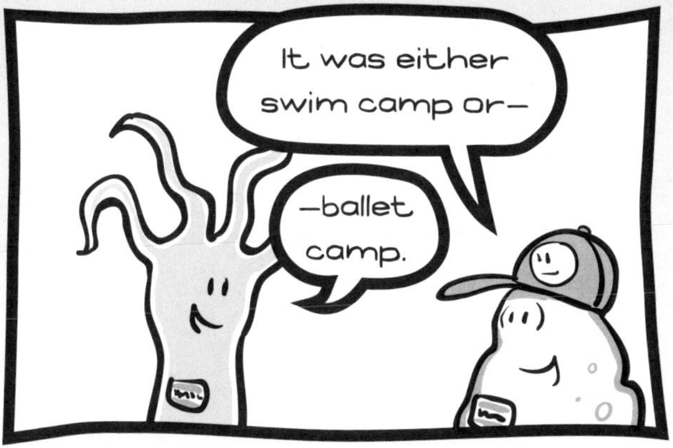
It was either swim camp or—
—ballet camp.

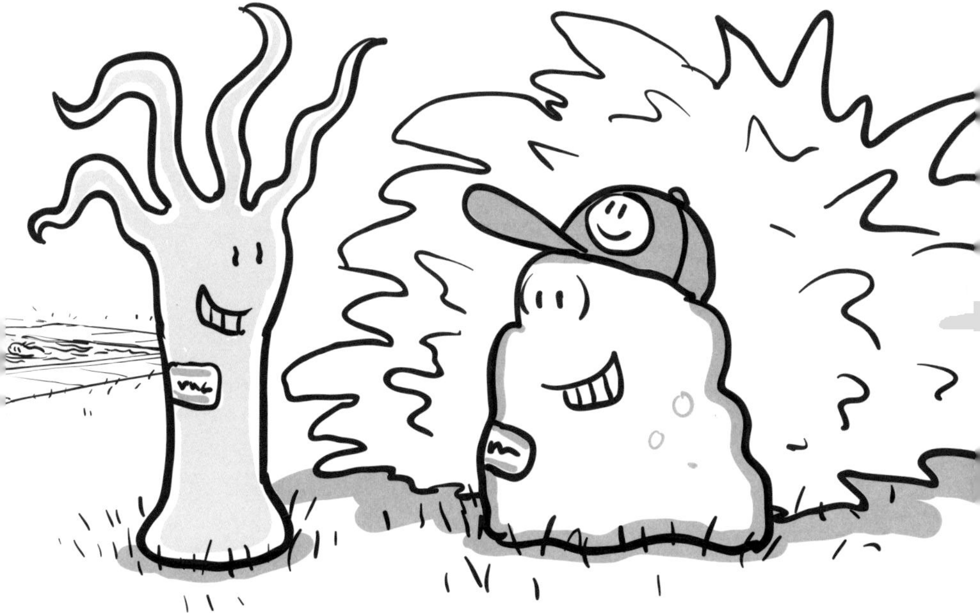

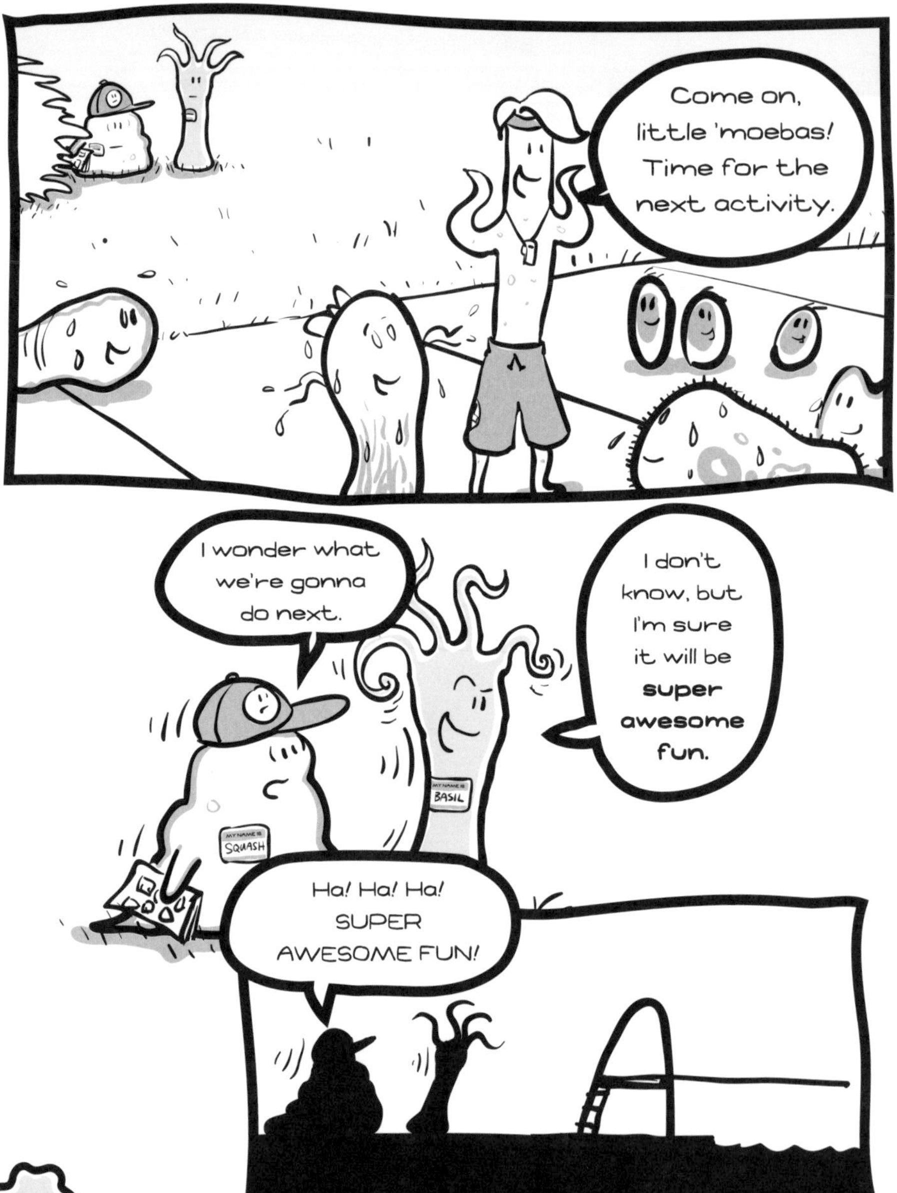
Come on, little 'moebas! Time for the next activity.
I wonder what we're gonna do next.
I don't know, but I'm sure it will be **super awesome fun.**
MY NAME IS BASIL
MY NAME IS SQUASH
Ha! Ha! Ha! SUPER AWESOME FUN!

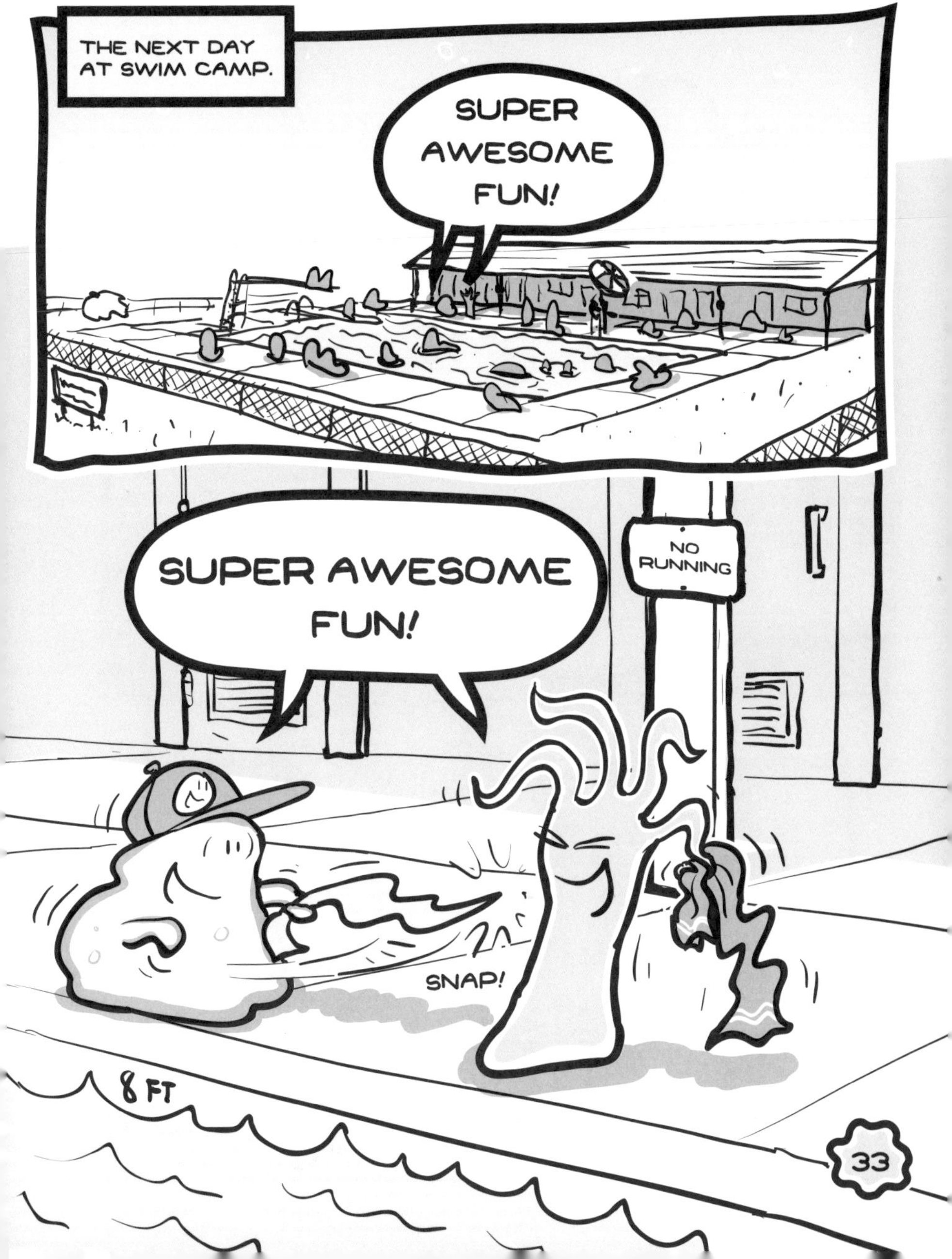

THE NEXT DAY AT SWIM CAMP.
SUPER AWESOME FUN!
NO RUNNING
SUPER AWESOME FUN!
SNAP!
8 FT

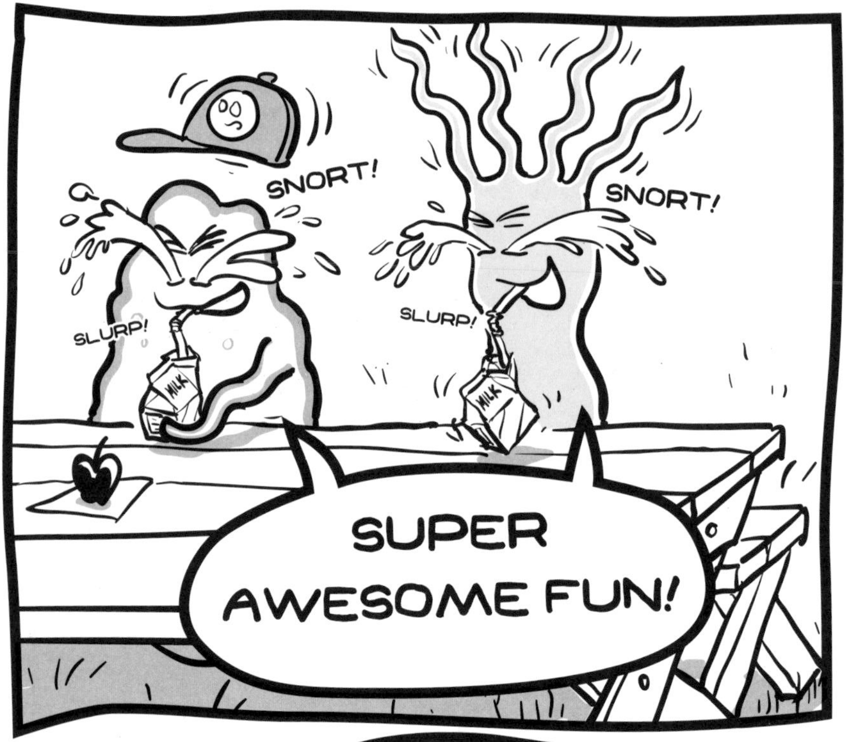
SNORT!
SNORT!
SLURP!
SLURP!
MILK
MILK
SUPER AWESOME FUN!

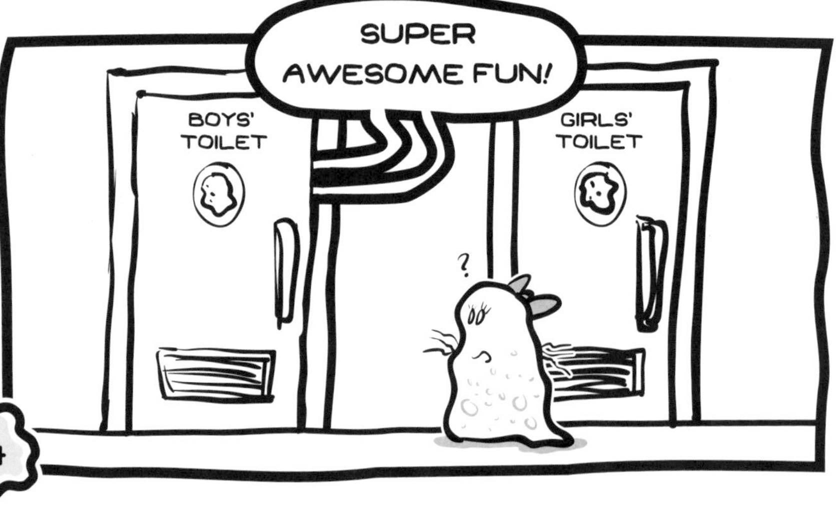
SUPER AWESOME FUN!
BOYS' TOILET
GIRLS' TOILET
?

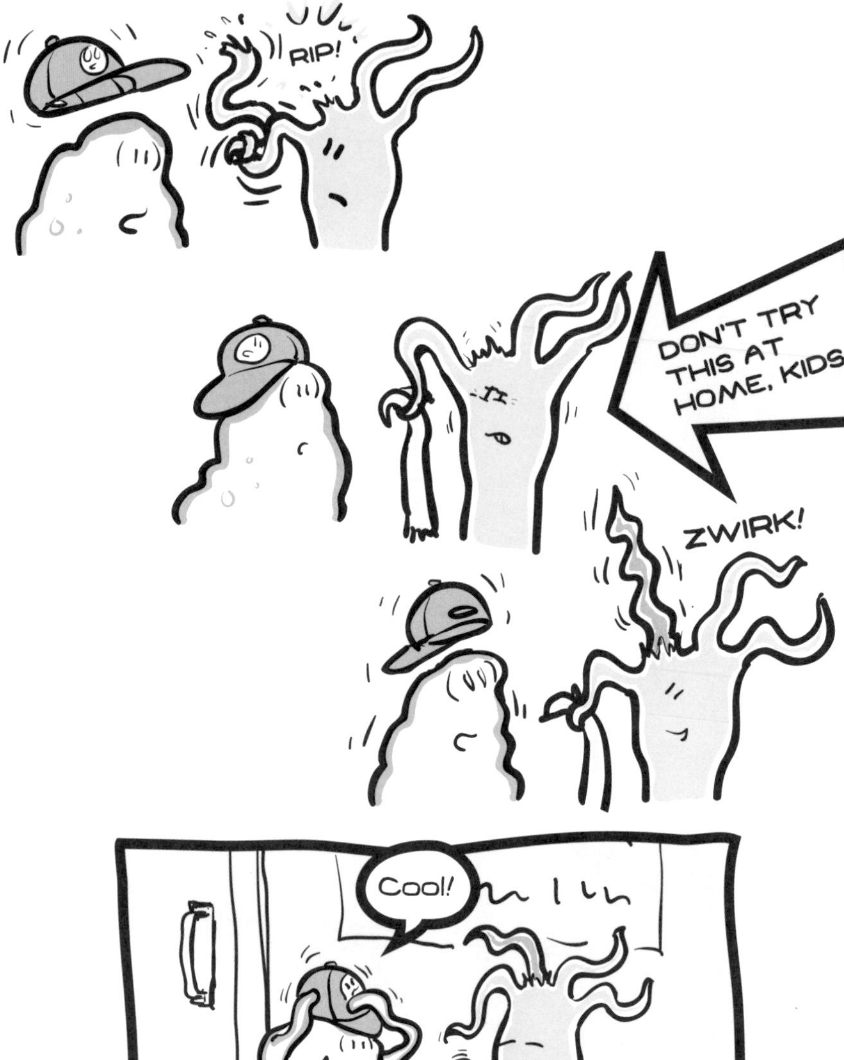
RIP!
DON'T TRY THIS AT HOME, KIDS!
ZWIRK!
Cool!

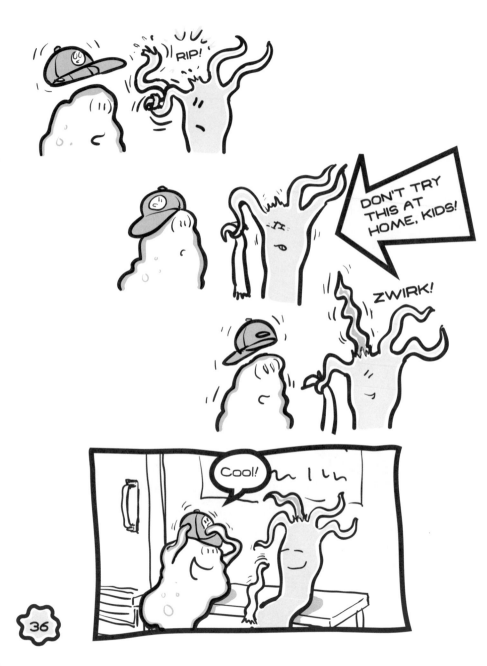

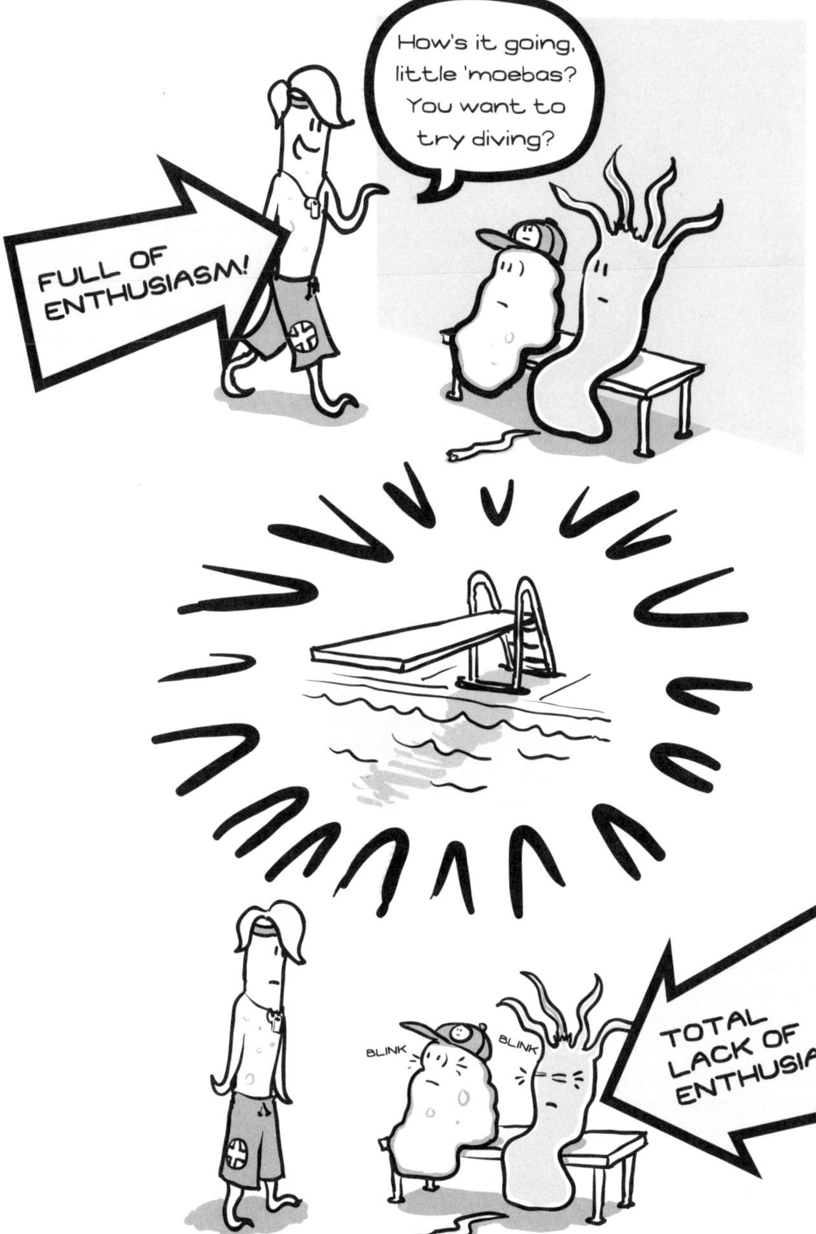
How's it going, little 'moebas? You want to try diving?
FULL OF ENTHUSIASM!
BLINK
BLINK
TOTAL LACK OF ENTHUSIASM.

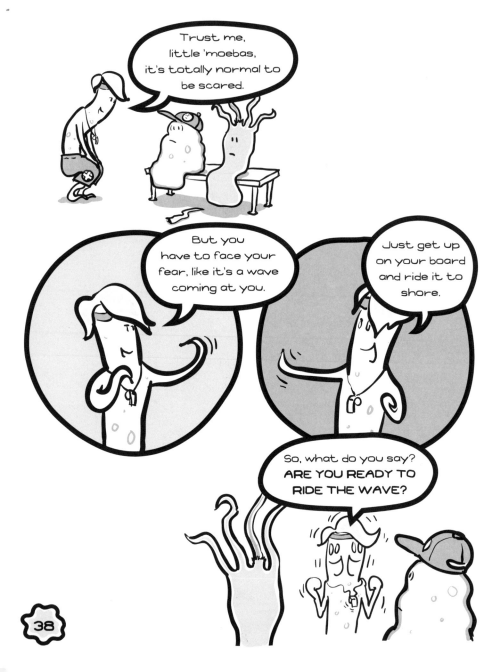

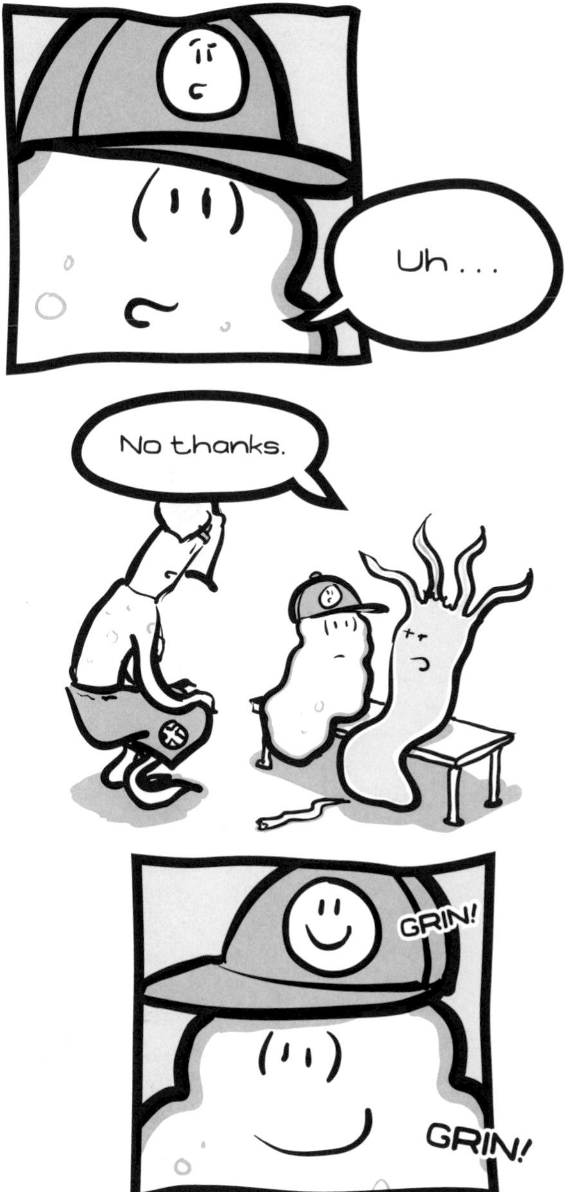
Uh . . .
No thanks.
GRIN!
GRIN!

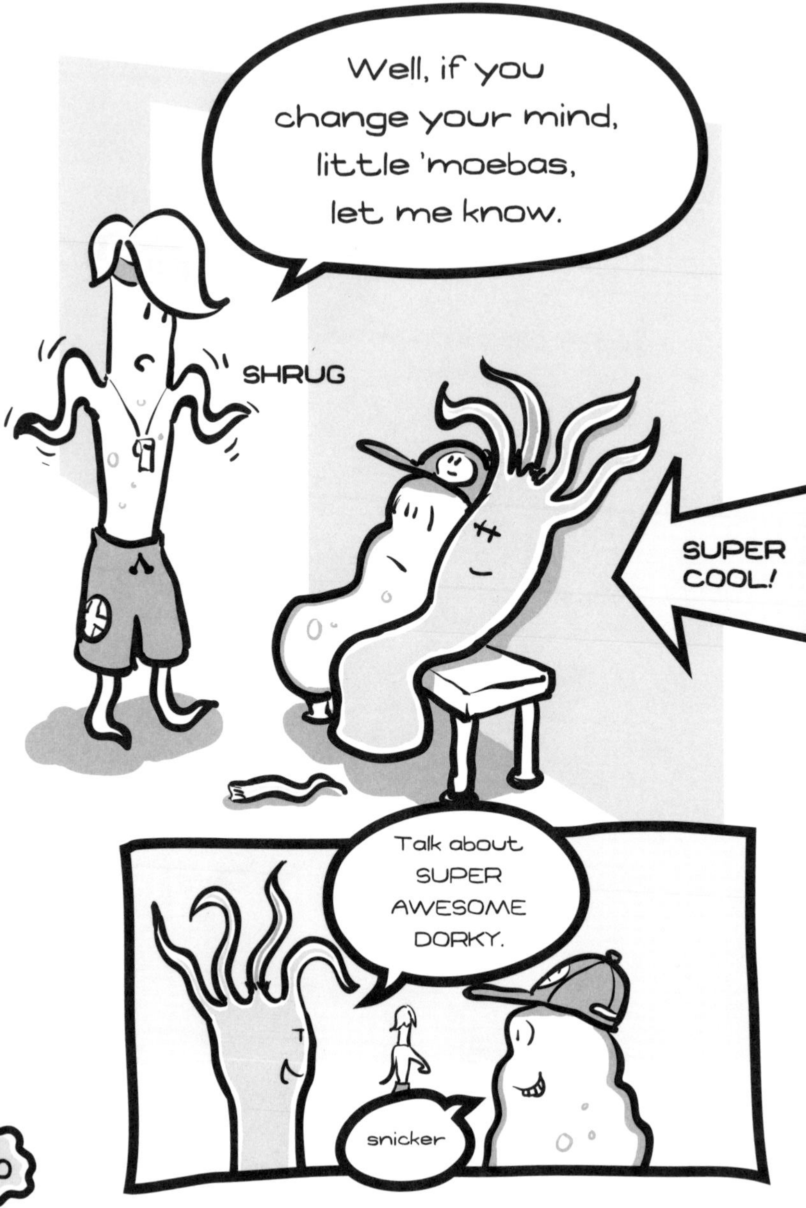
Well, if you change your mind, little 'moebas, let me know.
SHRUG
SUPER COOL!
Talk about SUPER AWESOME DORKY.
snicker

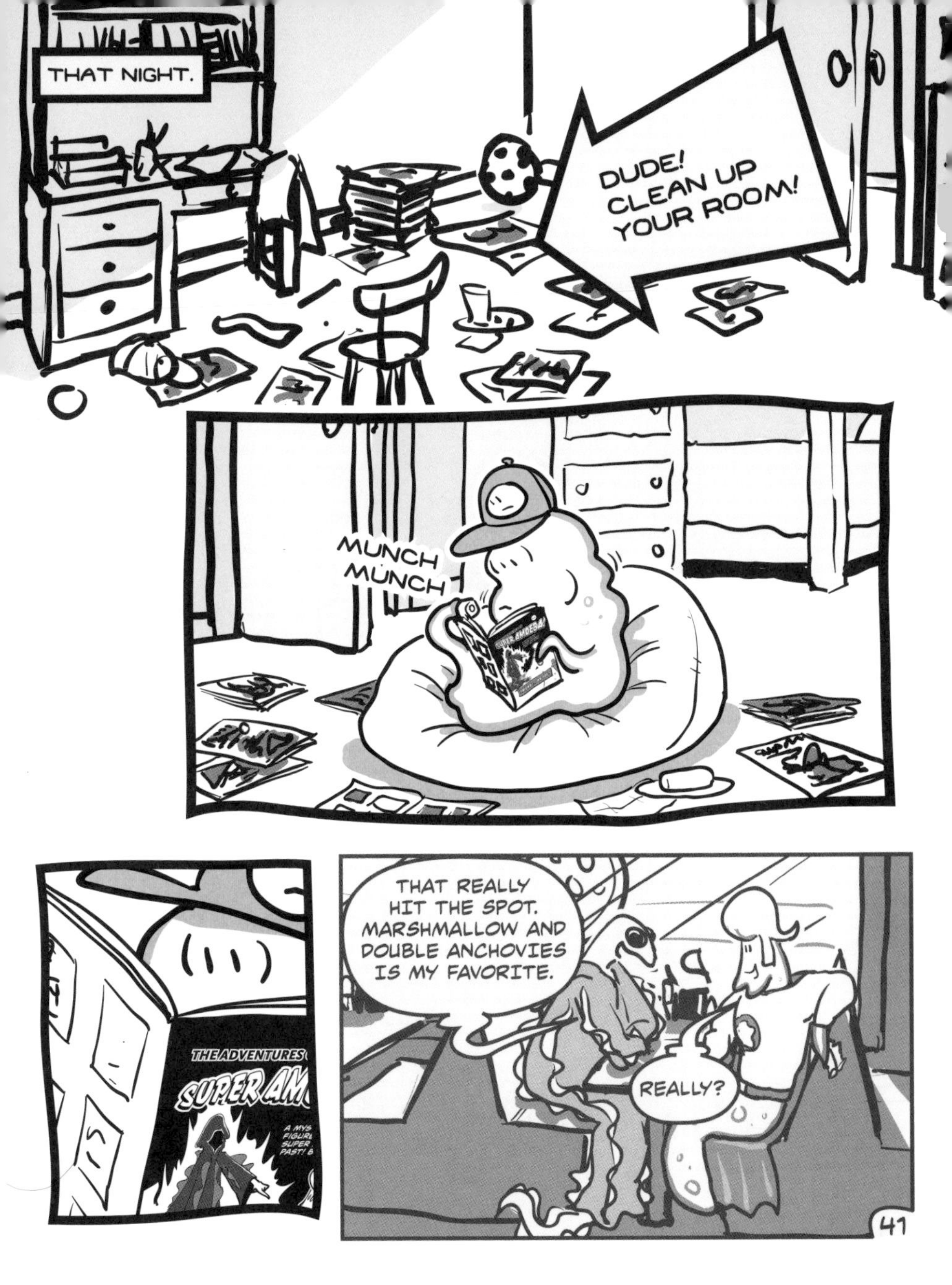
THAT NIGHT.
DUDE! CLEAN UP YOUR ROOM!
MUNCH MUNCH
THAT REALLY HIT THE SPOT. MARSHMALLOW AND DOUBLE ANCHOVIES IS MY FAVORITE.
REALLY?

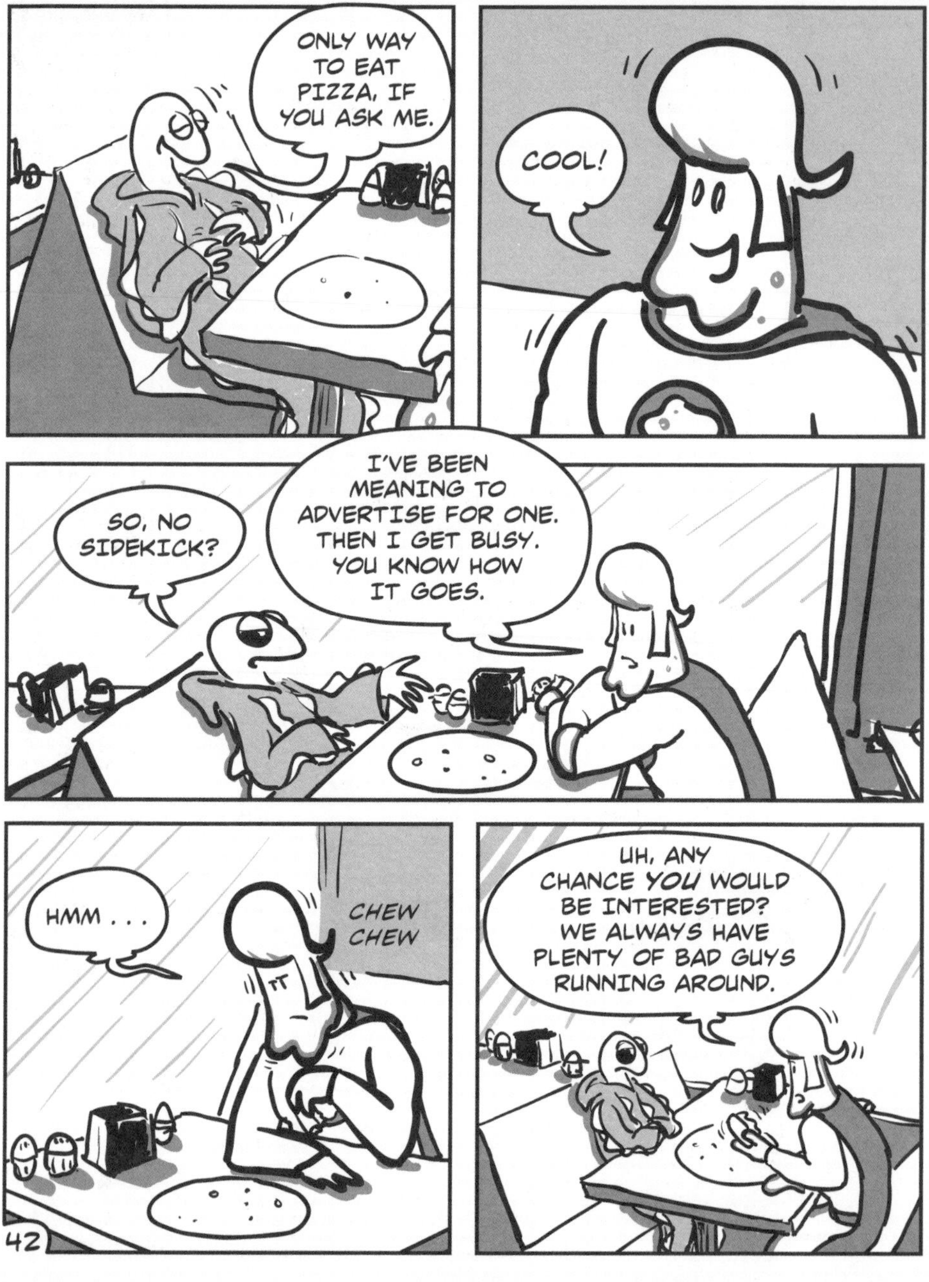
ONLY WAY TO EAT PIZZA, IF YOU ASK ME.
COOL!
SO, NO SIDEKICK?
I'VE BEEN MEANING TO ADVERTISE FOR ONE. THEN I GET BUSY. YOU KNOW HOW IT GOES.
HMM . . .
CHEW CHEW
UH, ANY CHANCE *YOU* WOULD BE INTERESTED? WE ALWAYS HAVE PLENTY OF BAD GUYS RUNNING AROUND.

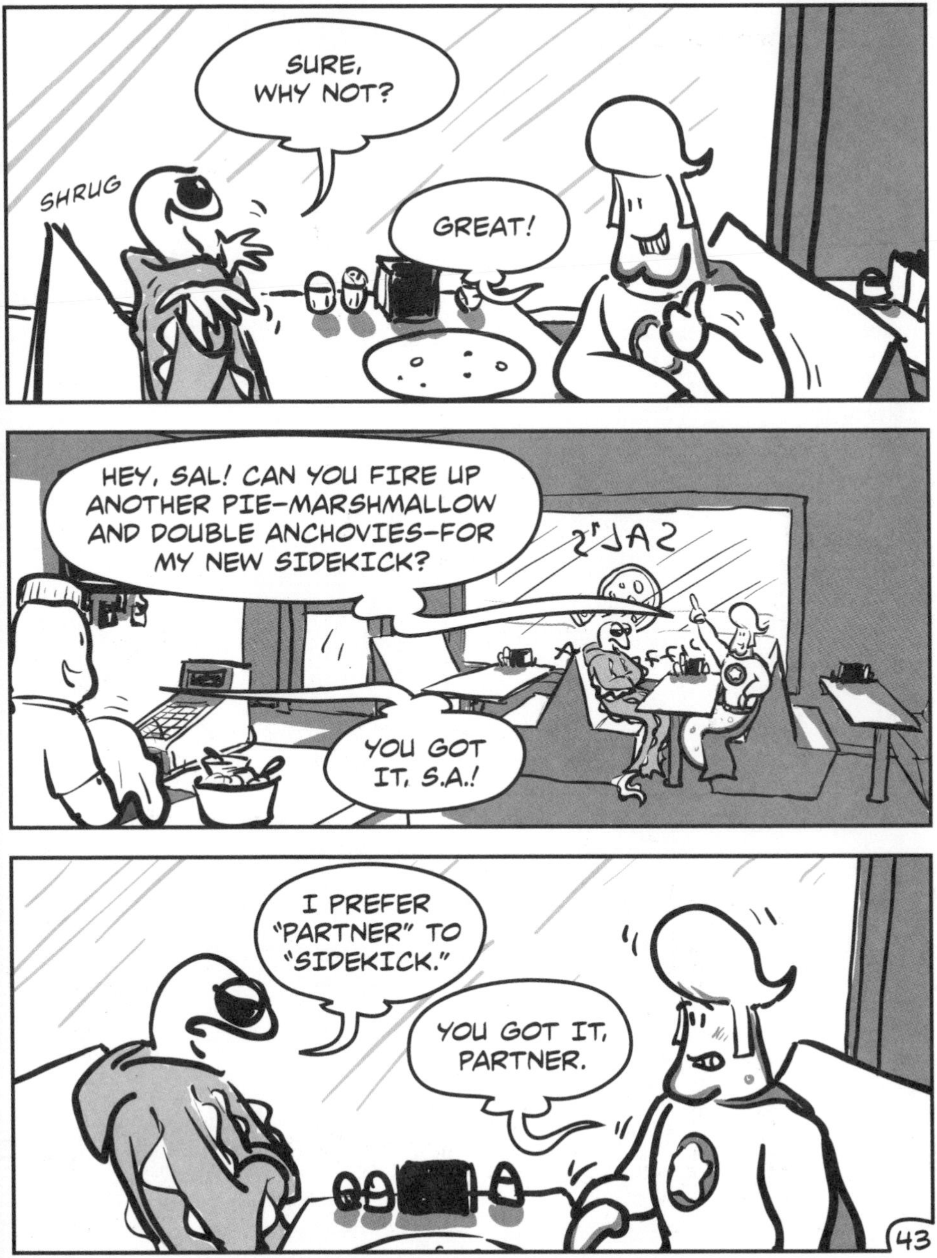
SHRUG
SURE, WHY NOT?
GREAT!
HEY, SAL! CAN YOU FIRE UP ANOTHER PIE—MARSHMALLOW AND DOUBLE ANCHOVIES—FOR MY NEW SIDEKICK?
YOU GOT IT, S.A.!
I PREFER "PARTNER" TO "SIDEKICK."
YOU GOT IT, PARTNER.

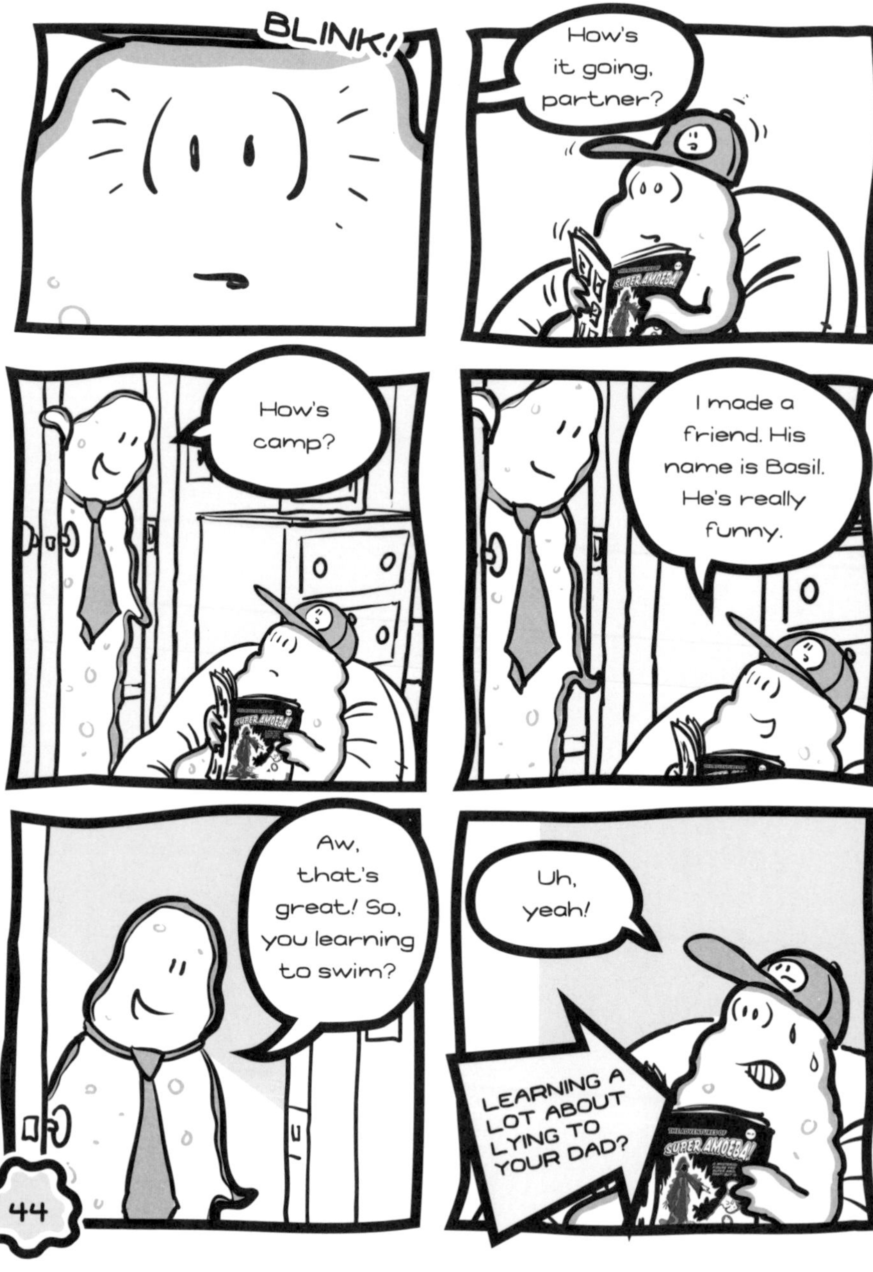
BLINK!
How's it going, partner?
How's camp?
I made a friend. His name is Basil. He's really funny.
Aw, that's great! So, you learning to swim?
Uh, yeah!
LEARNING A LOT ABOUT LYING TO YOUR DAD?
THE ADVENTURES OF SUPER AMOEBA!

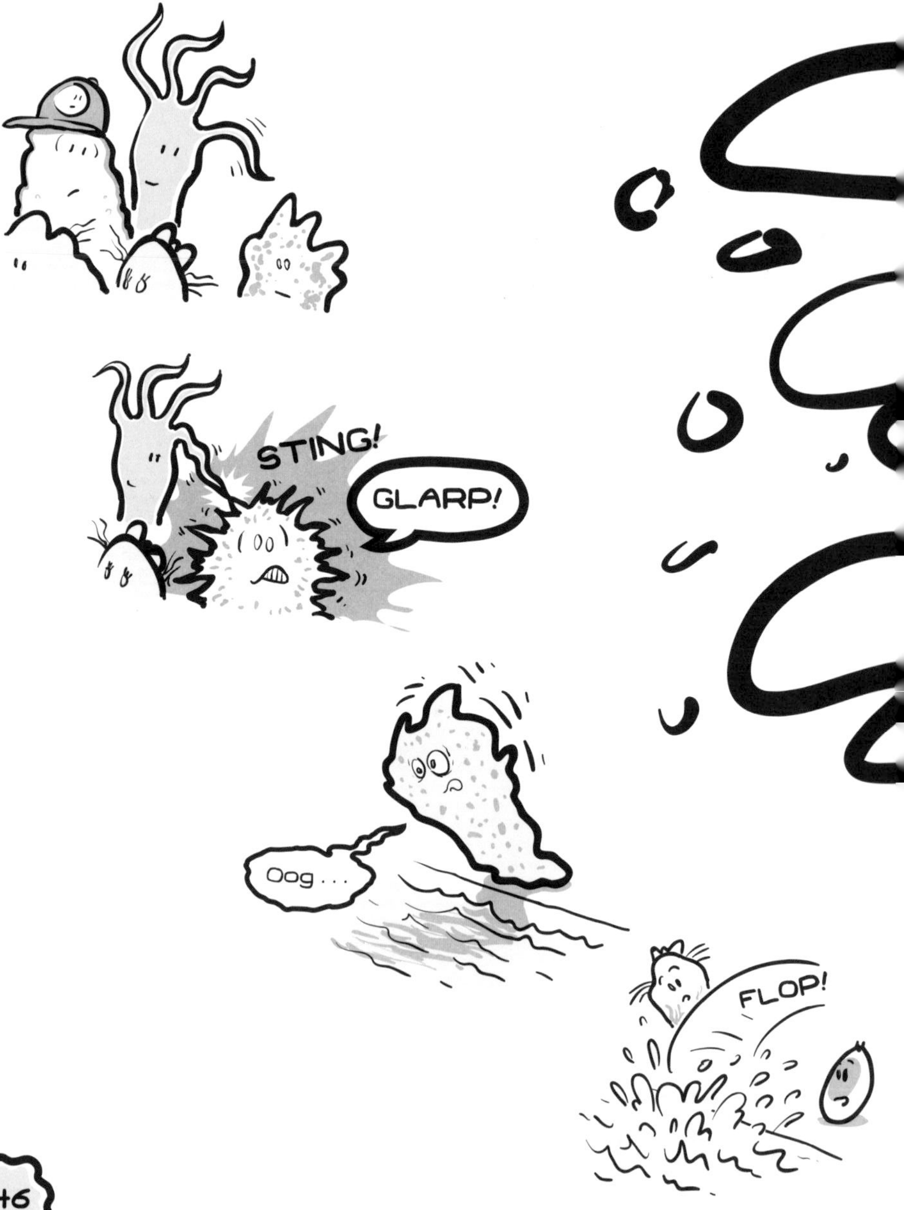
STING!
GLARP!
Oog . . .
FLOP!

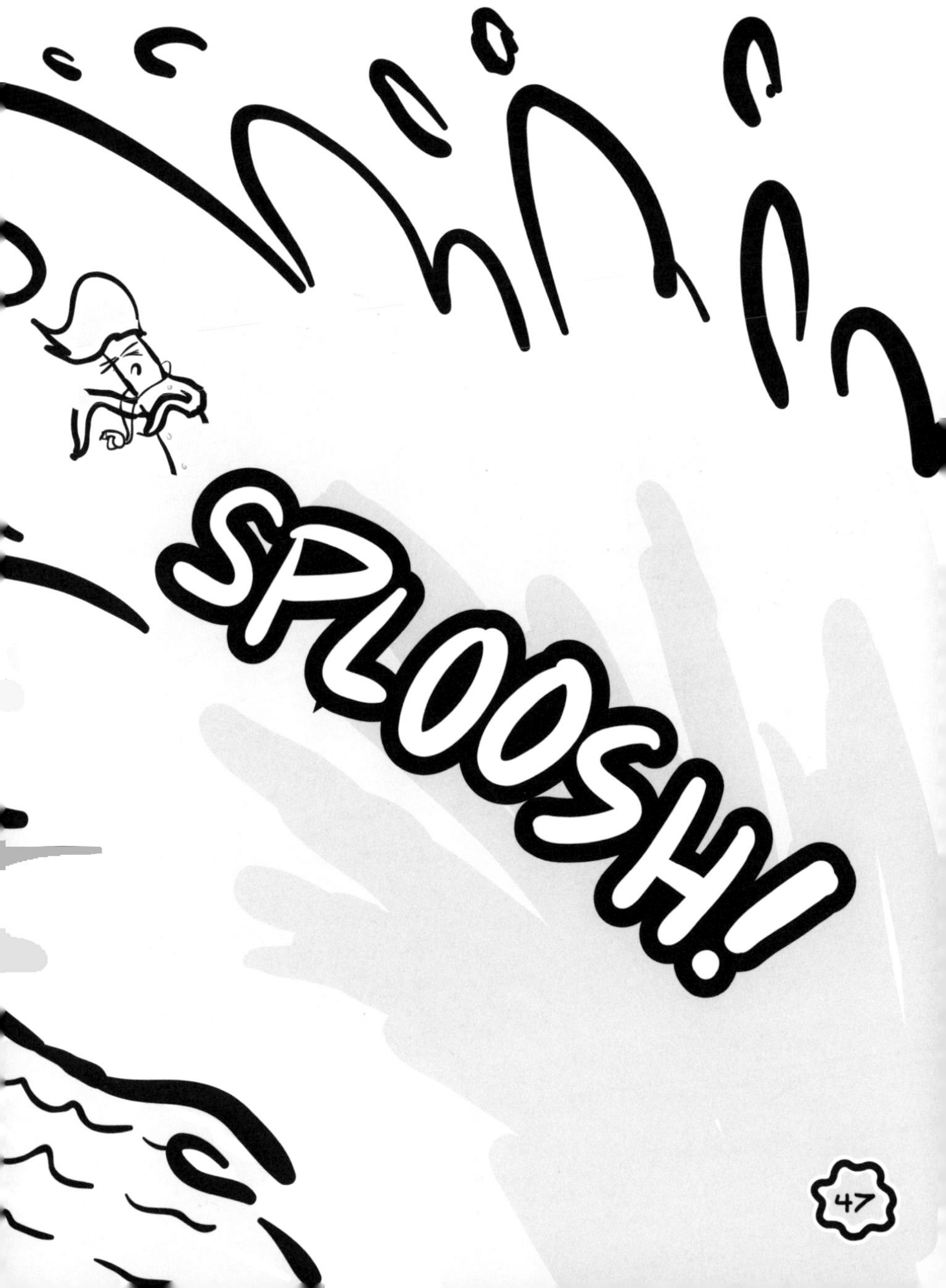
SPLOOSH!

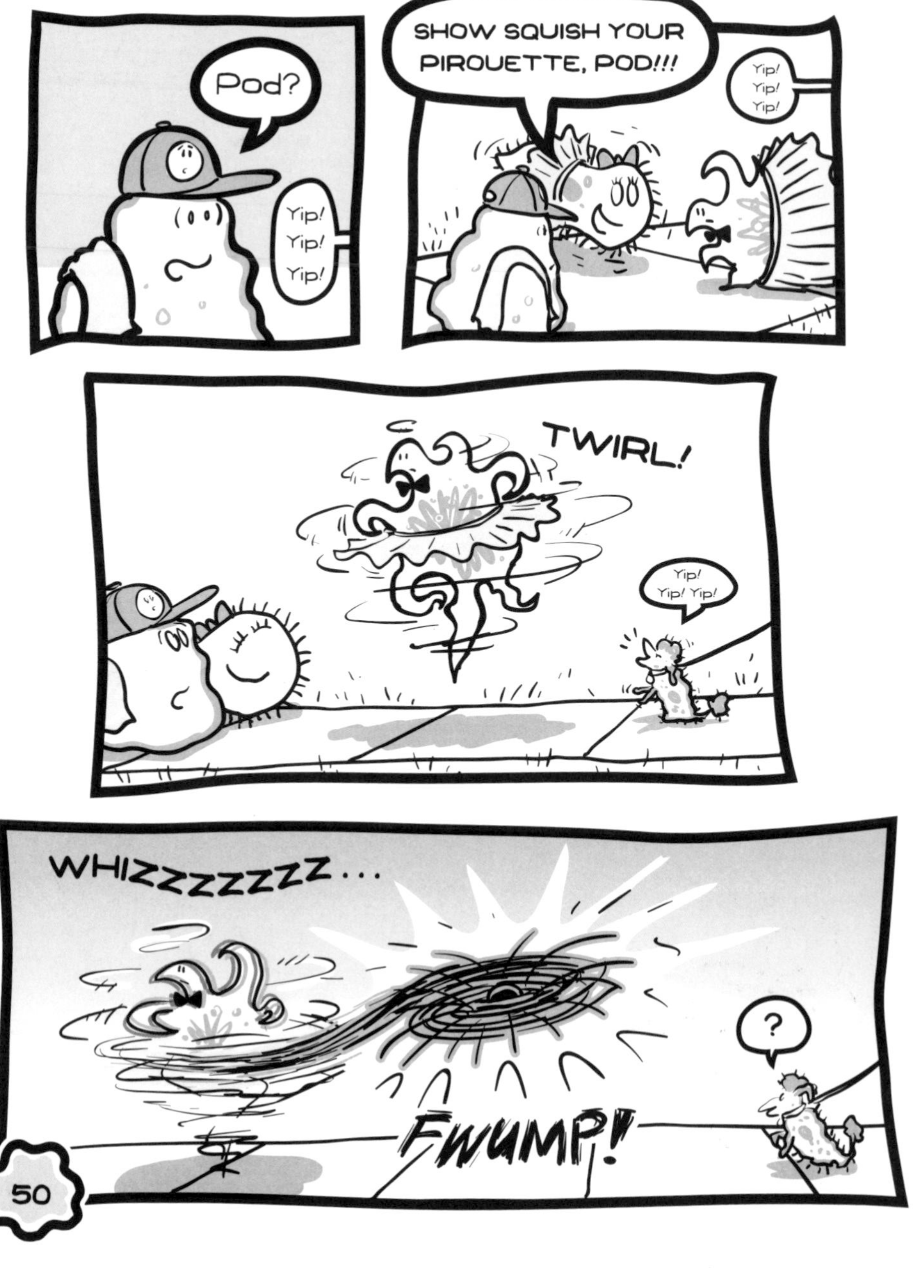
Pod?
Yip! Yip! Yip!
SHOW SQUISH YOUR PIROUETTE, POD!!!
Yip! Yip! Yip!
TWIRL!
Yip! Yip! Yip!
WHIZZZZZZZZ...
?
FWUMP!

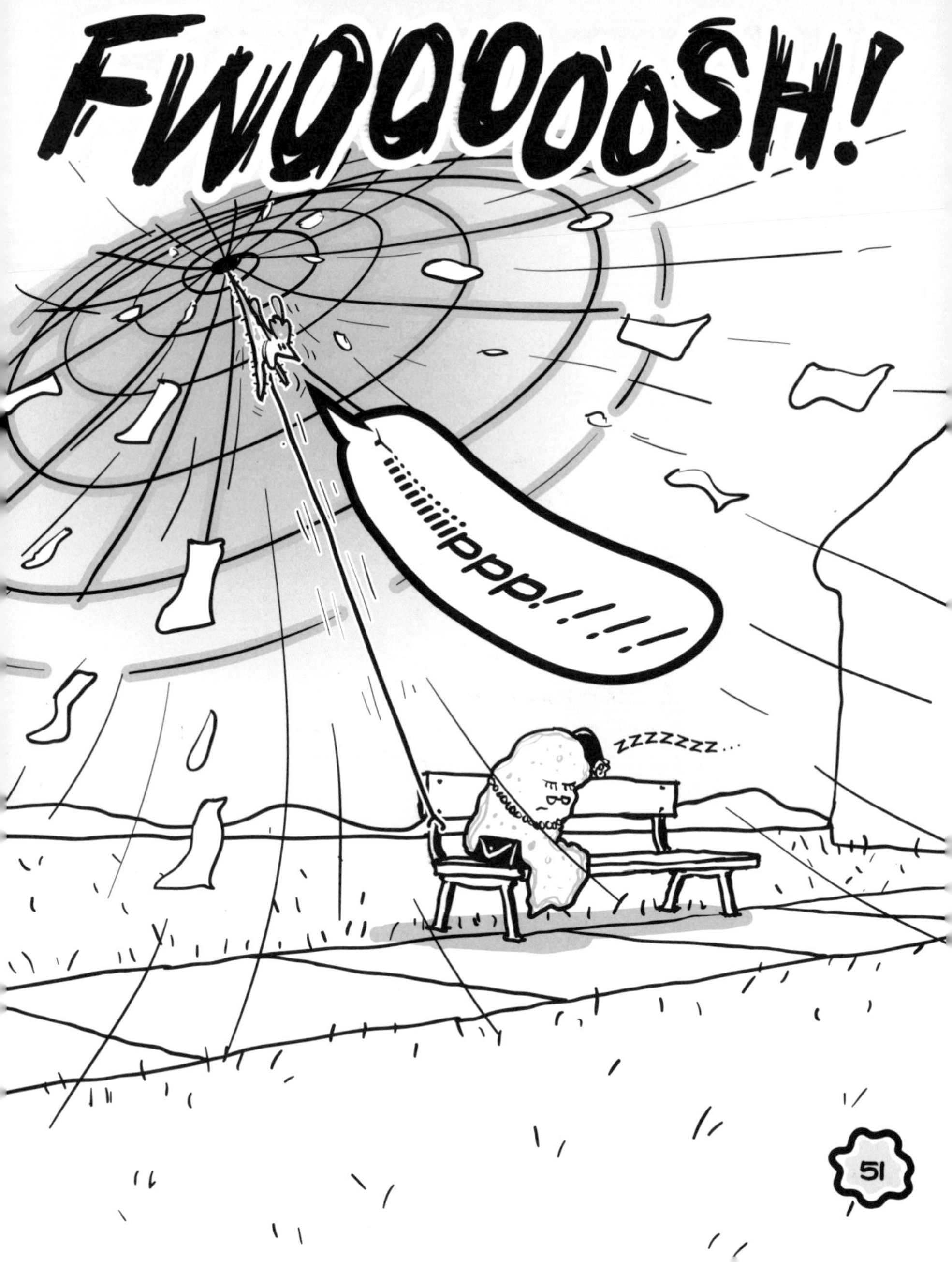
FWOOOOOSH!
Yiiiiiiiiiiippp!!!!!
zzzzzzz...

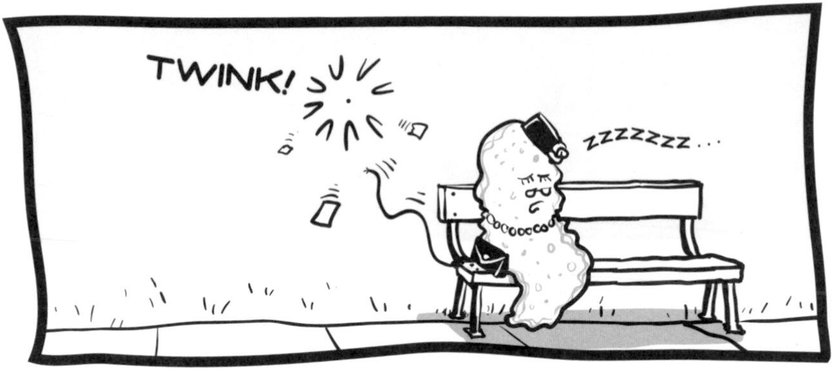
TWINK!
ZZZZZZZ...

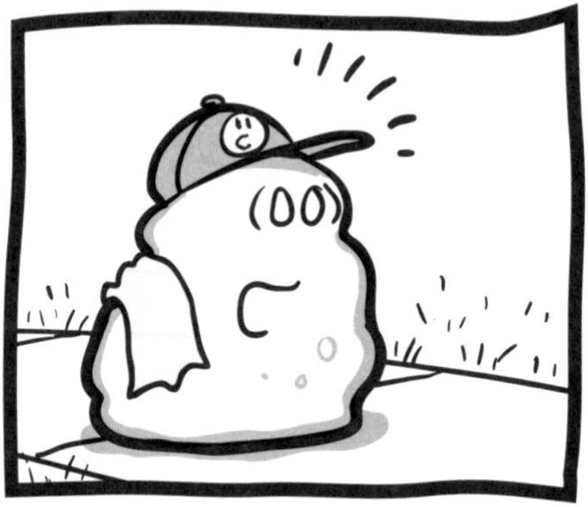

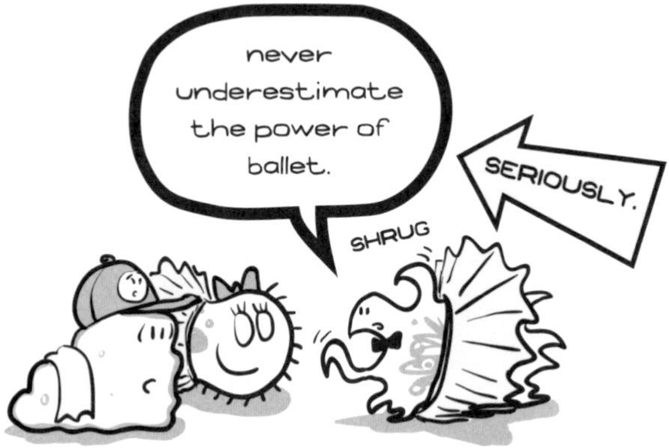
never underestimate the power of ballet.
SERIOUSLY.
SHRUG

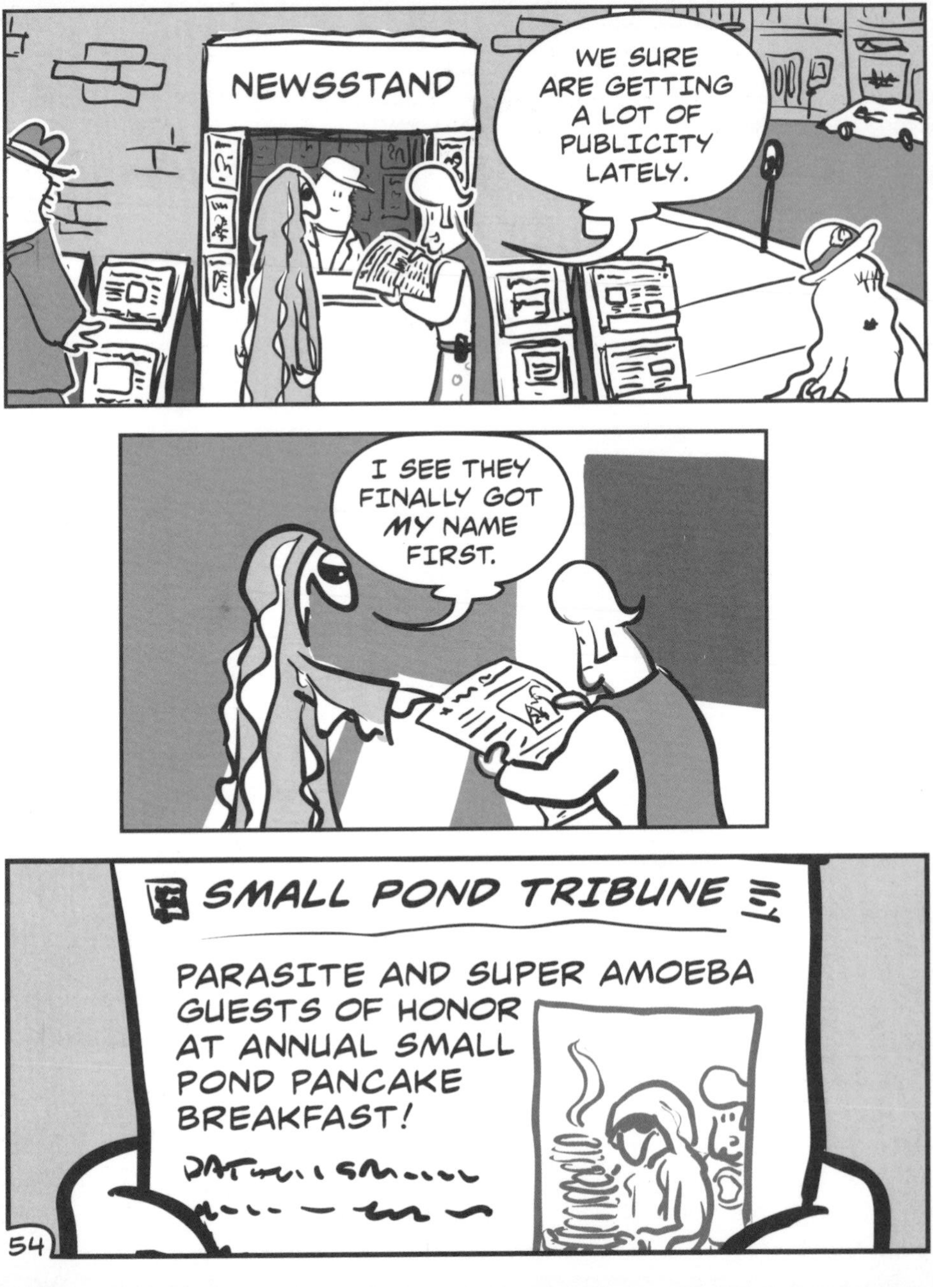
NEWSSTAND
WE SURE ARE GETTING A LOT OF PUBLICITY LATELY.
I SEE THEY FINALLY GOT *MY* NAME FIRST.
SMALL POND TRIBUNE
PARASITE AND SUPER AMOEBA GUESTS OF HONOR AT ANNUAL SMALL POND PANCAKE BREAKFAST!

BEEP!
BEEP!

?

BEEP!
BEEP!

CLICK

PARASITE HERE.

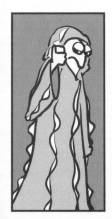

SORRY, MAYOR. WE'RE SUPERHEROES. WE DON'T RESCUE CATS FROM TREES.

I'M HUNGRY. LET'S GET LUNCH.

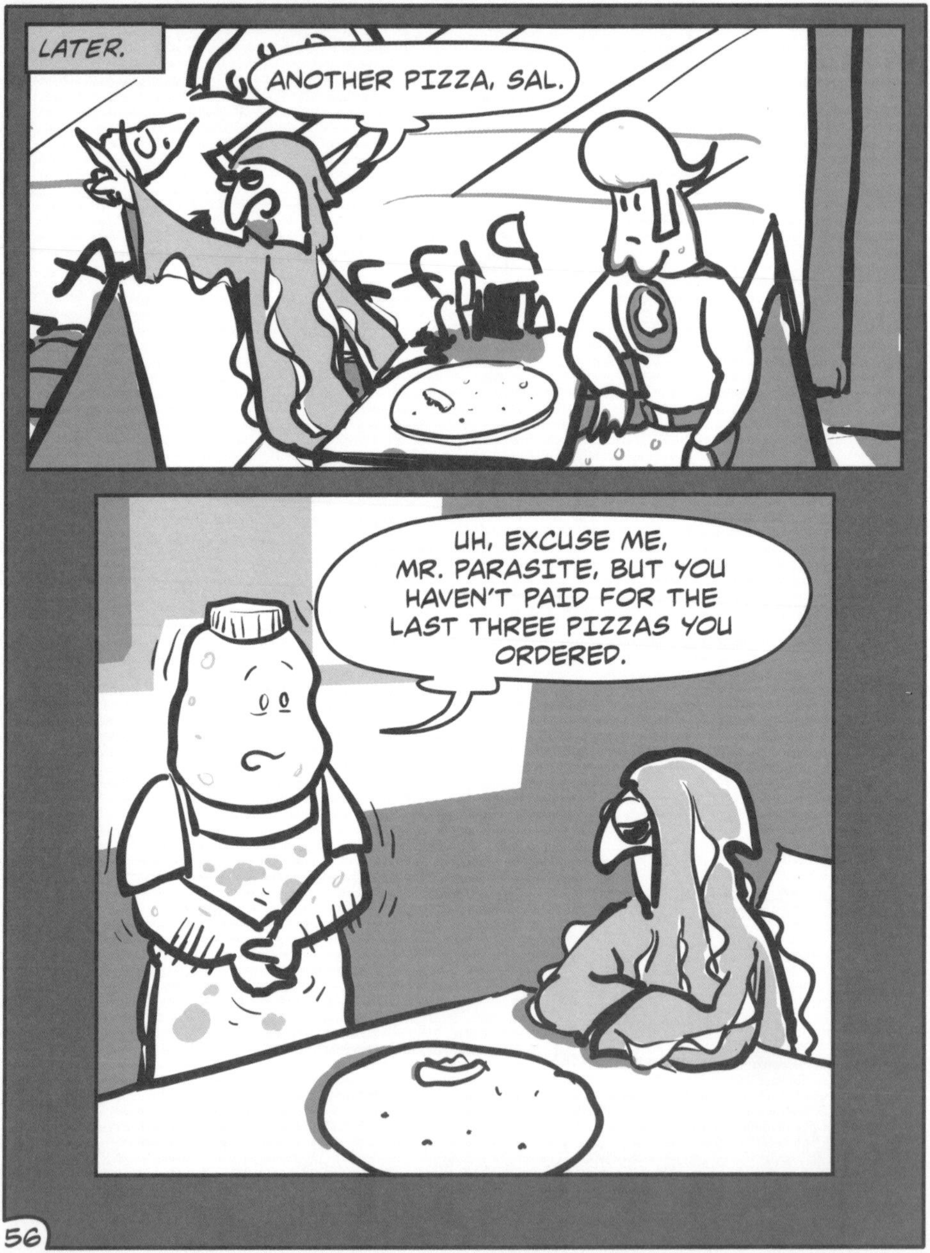

LATER.
ANOTHER PIZZA, SAL.
UH, EXCUSE ME, MR. PARASITE, BUT YOU HAVEN'T PAID FOR THE LAST THREE PIZZAS YOU ORDERED.

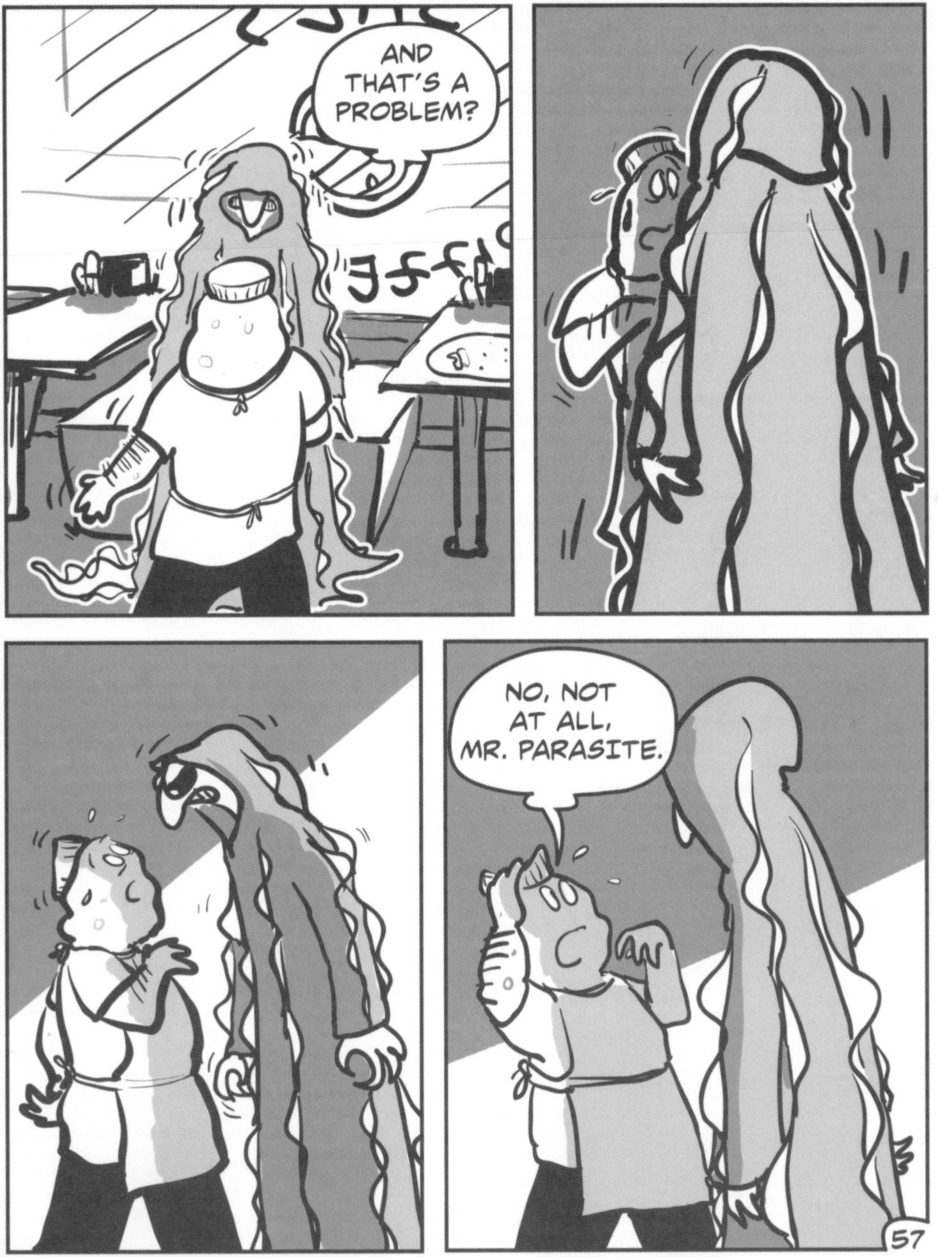
AND THAT'S A PROBLEM?
NO, NOT AT ALL, MR. PARASITE.

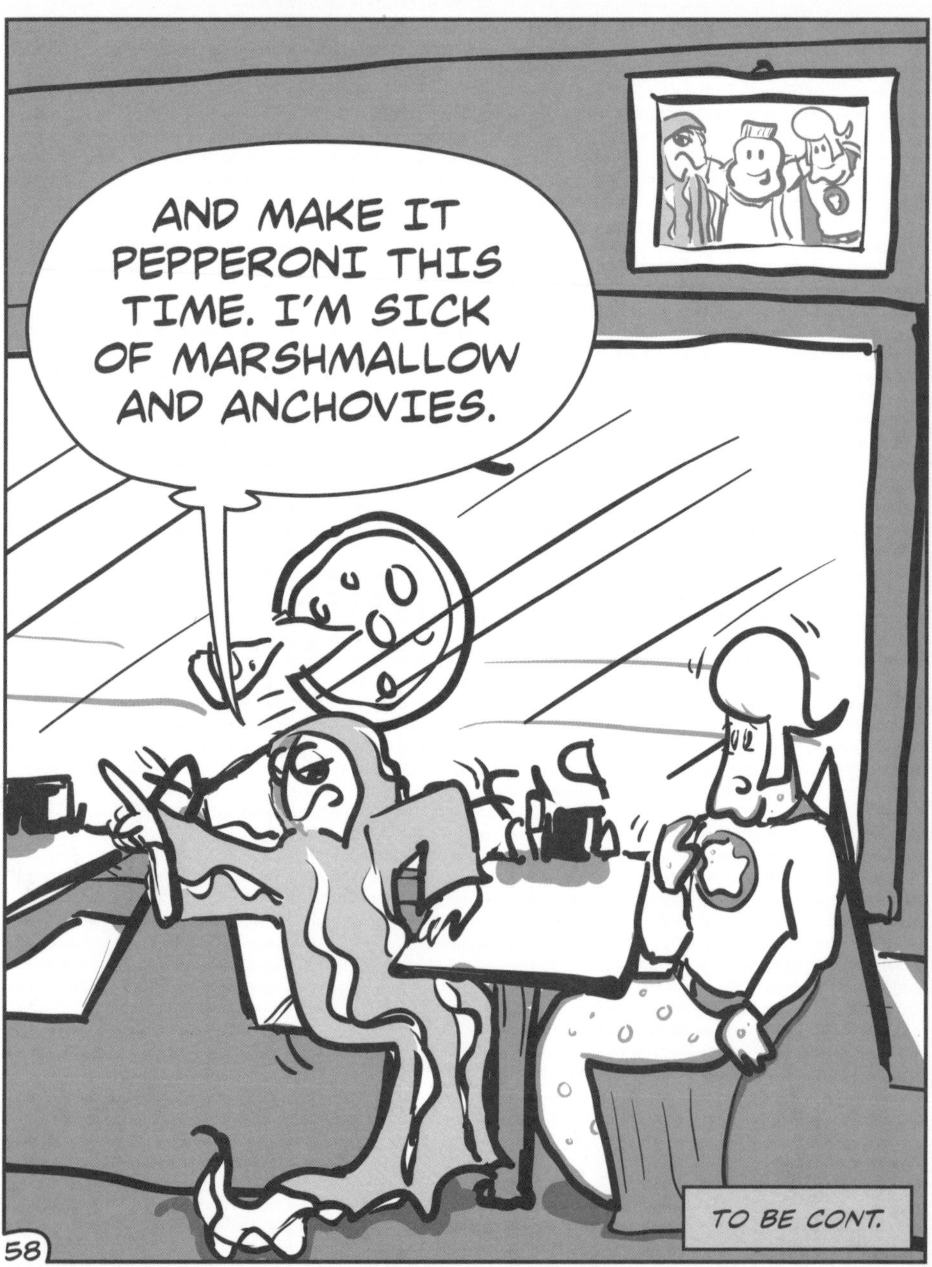
AND MAKE IT PEPPERONI THIS TIME. I'M SICK OF MARSHMALLOW AND ANCHOVIES.
TO BE CONT.

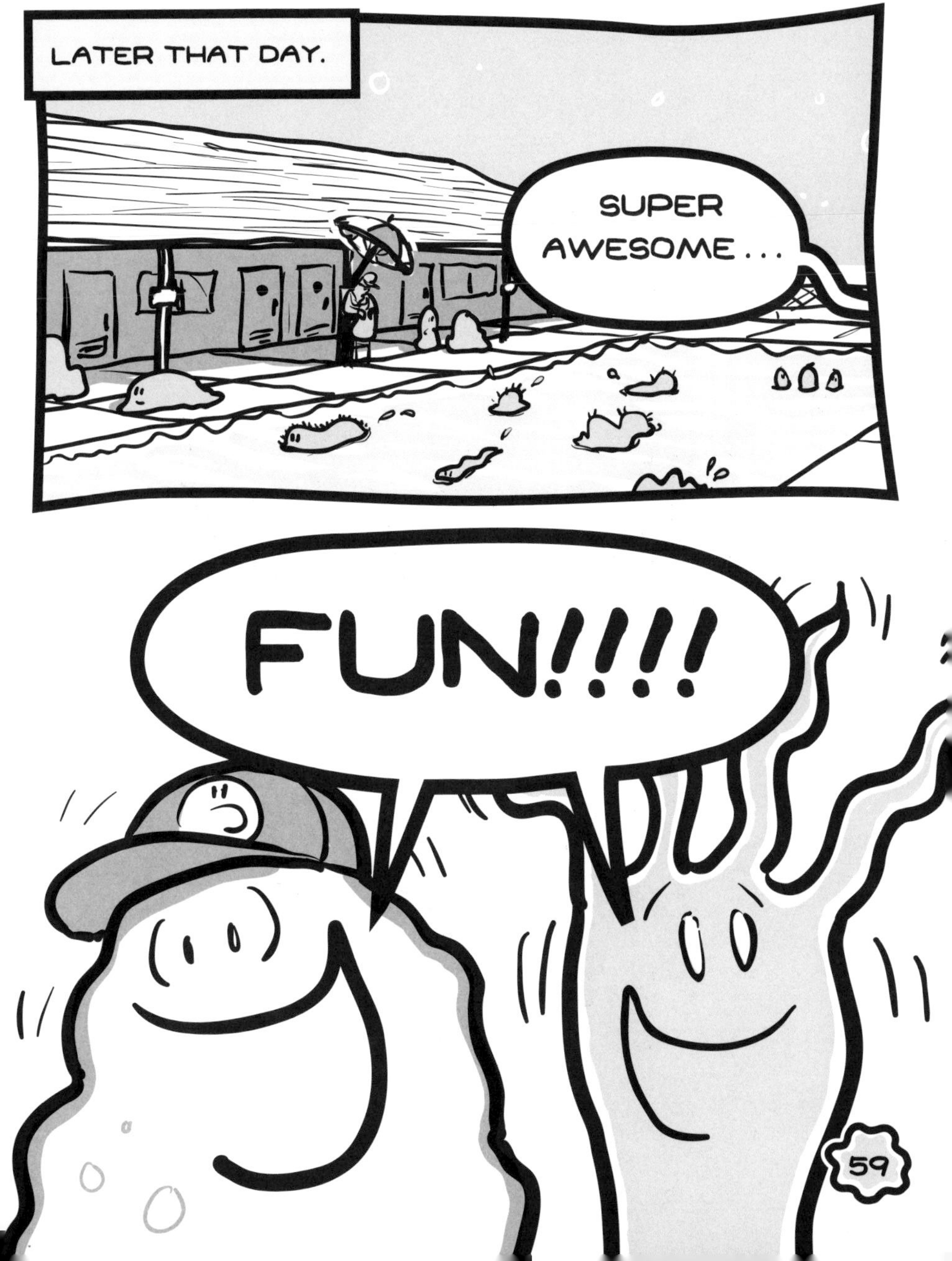
LATER THAT DAY.
SUPER AWESOME . . .
FUN!!!!

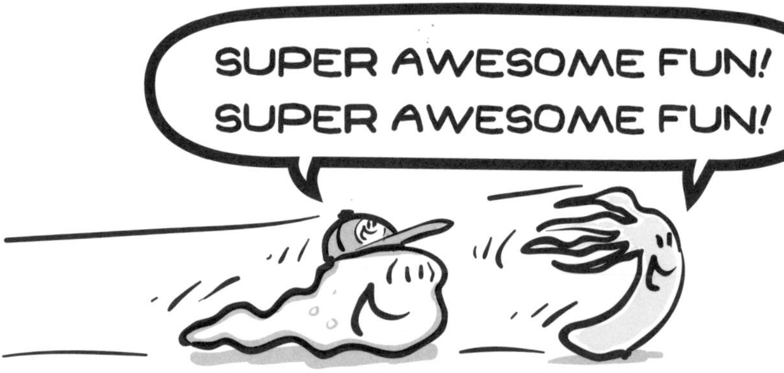
SUPER AWESOME FUN!
SUPER AWESOME FUN!

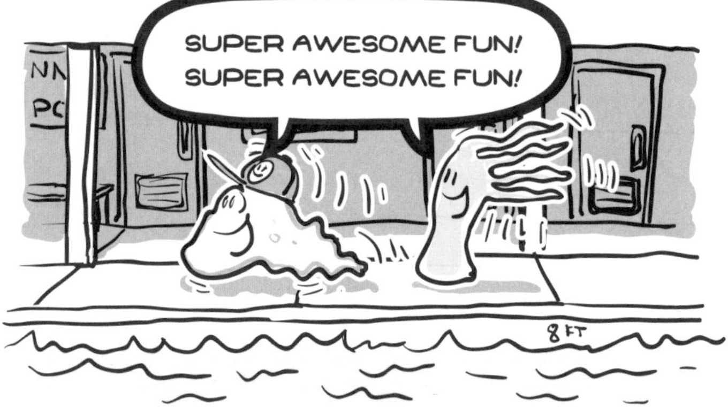
SUPER AWESOME FUN!
SUPER AWESOME FUN!
8 FT

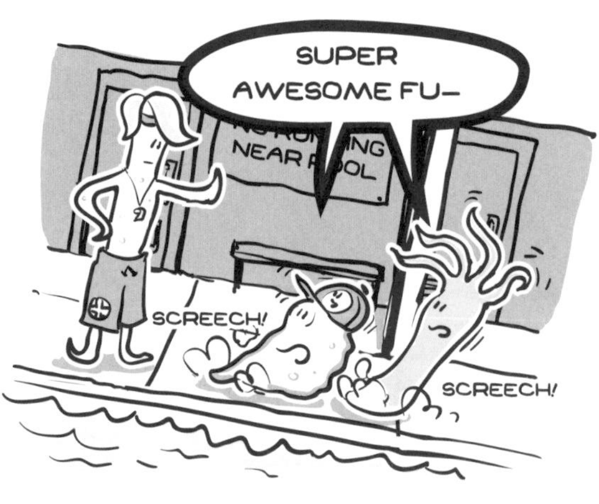
SUPER
AWESOME FU—
NEAR
SCREECH!
SCREECH!

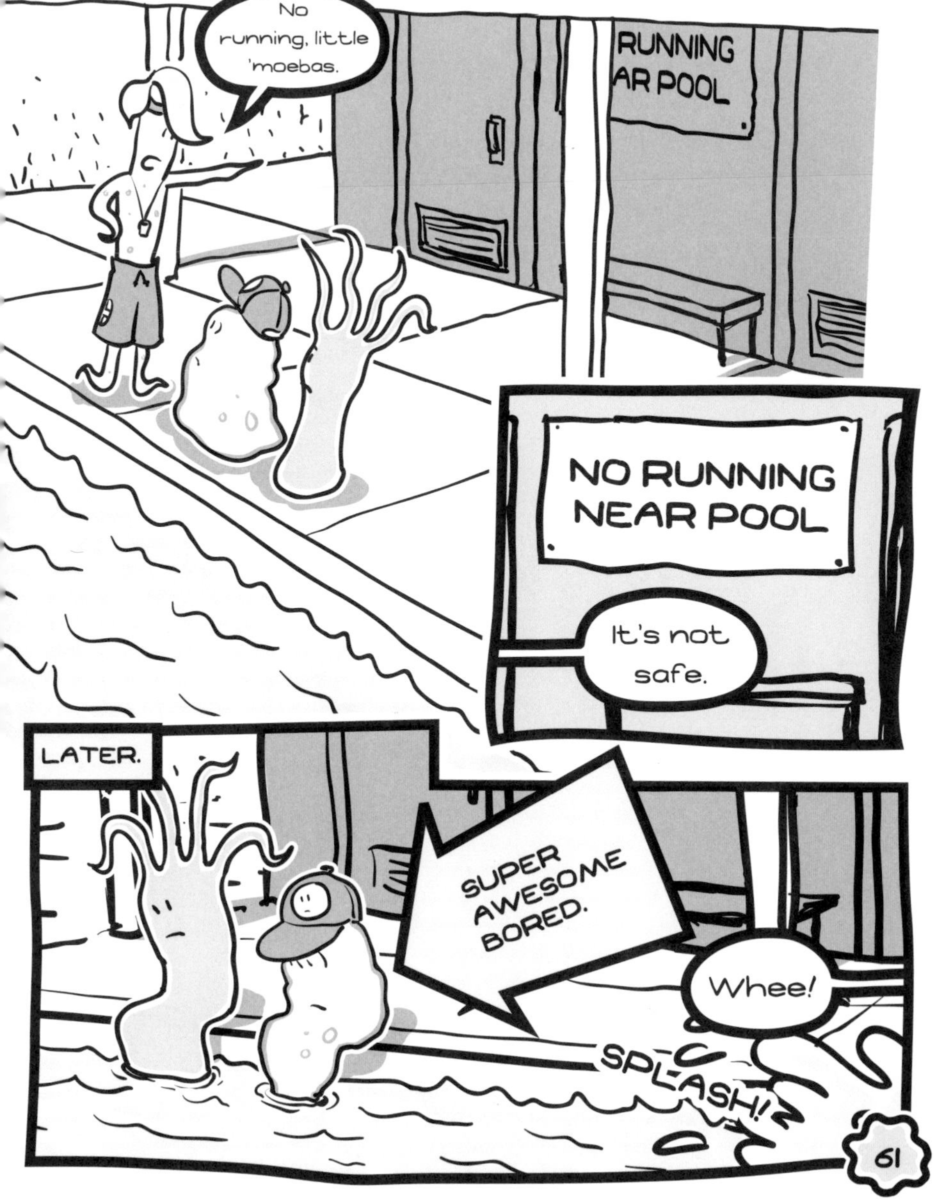
No running, little 'moebas.
RUNNING
AR POOL
NO RUNNING NEAR POOL
It's not safe.
LATER.
SUPER AWESOME BORED.
Whee!
SPLASH!

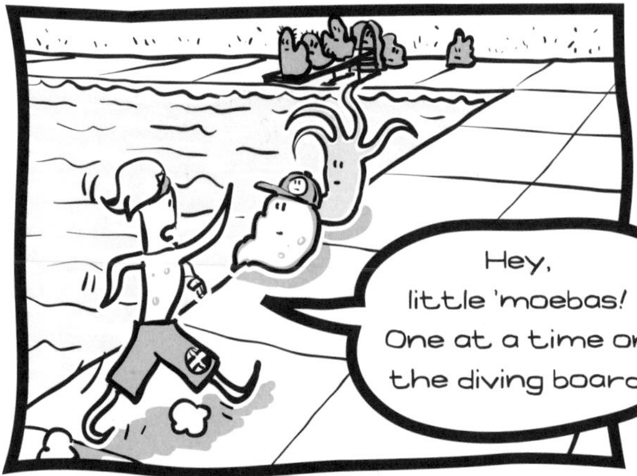
Hey, little 'moebas! One at a time on the diving board.

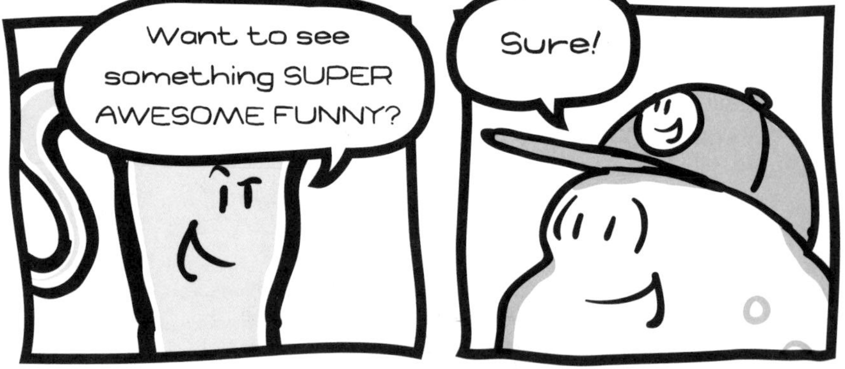
Want to see something SUPER AWESOME FUNNY?
Sure!

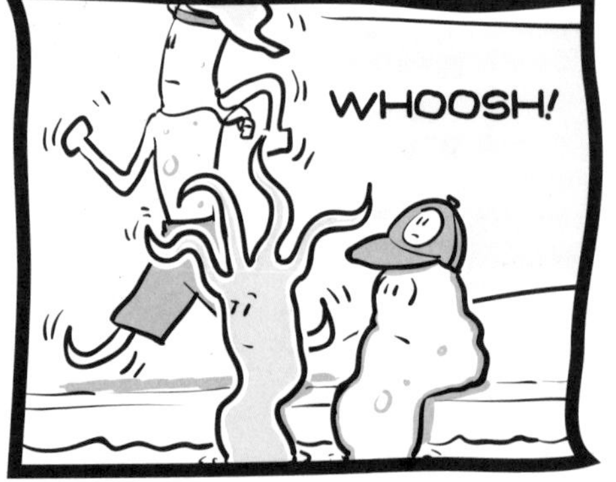
WHOOSH!

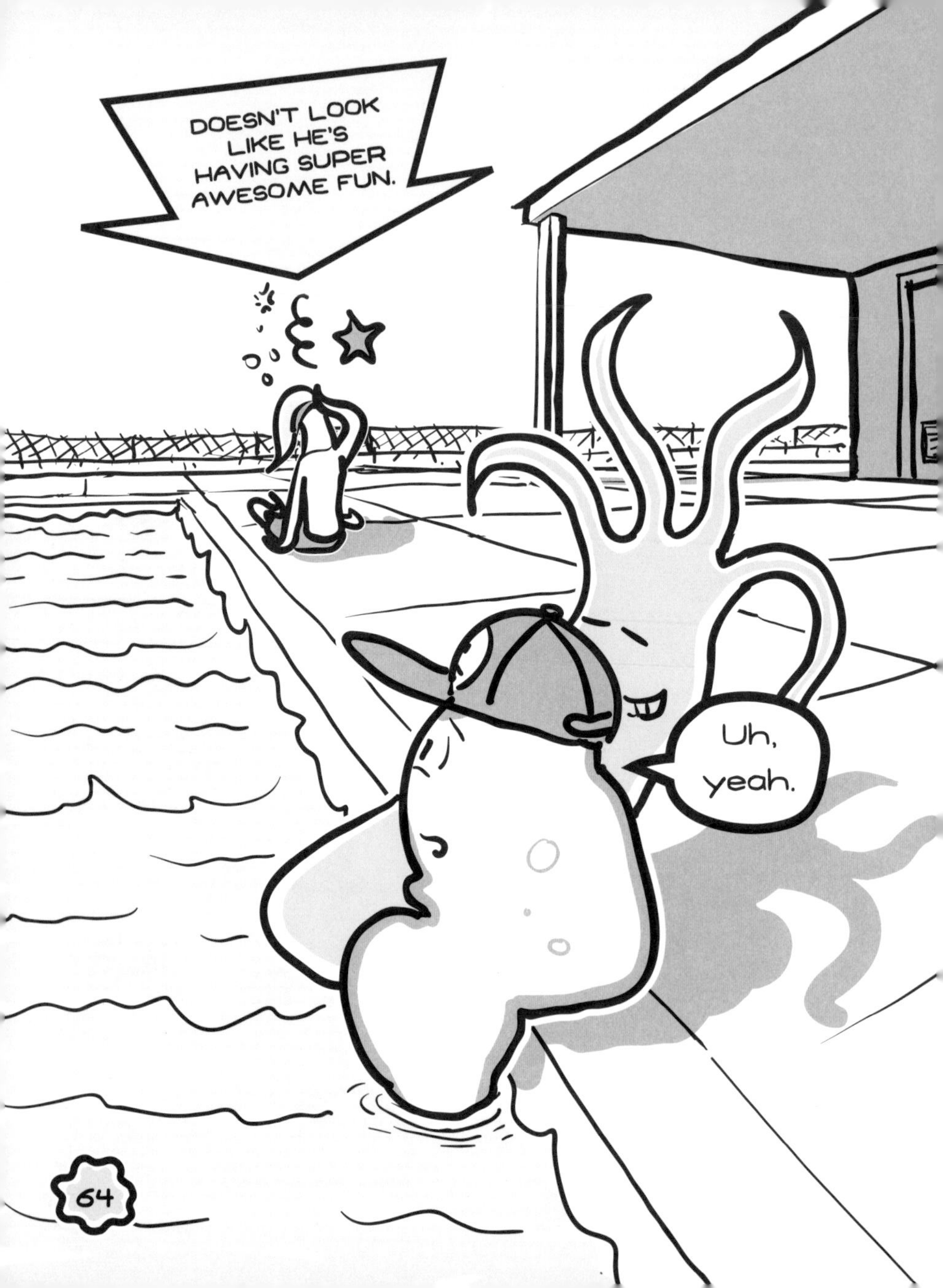
DOESN'T LOOK LIKE HE'S HAVING SUPER AWESOME FUN.
Uh, yeah.

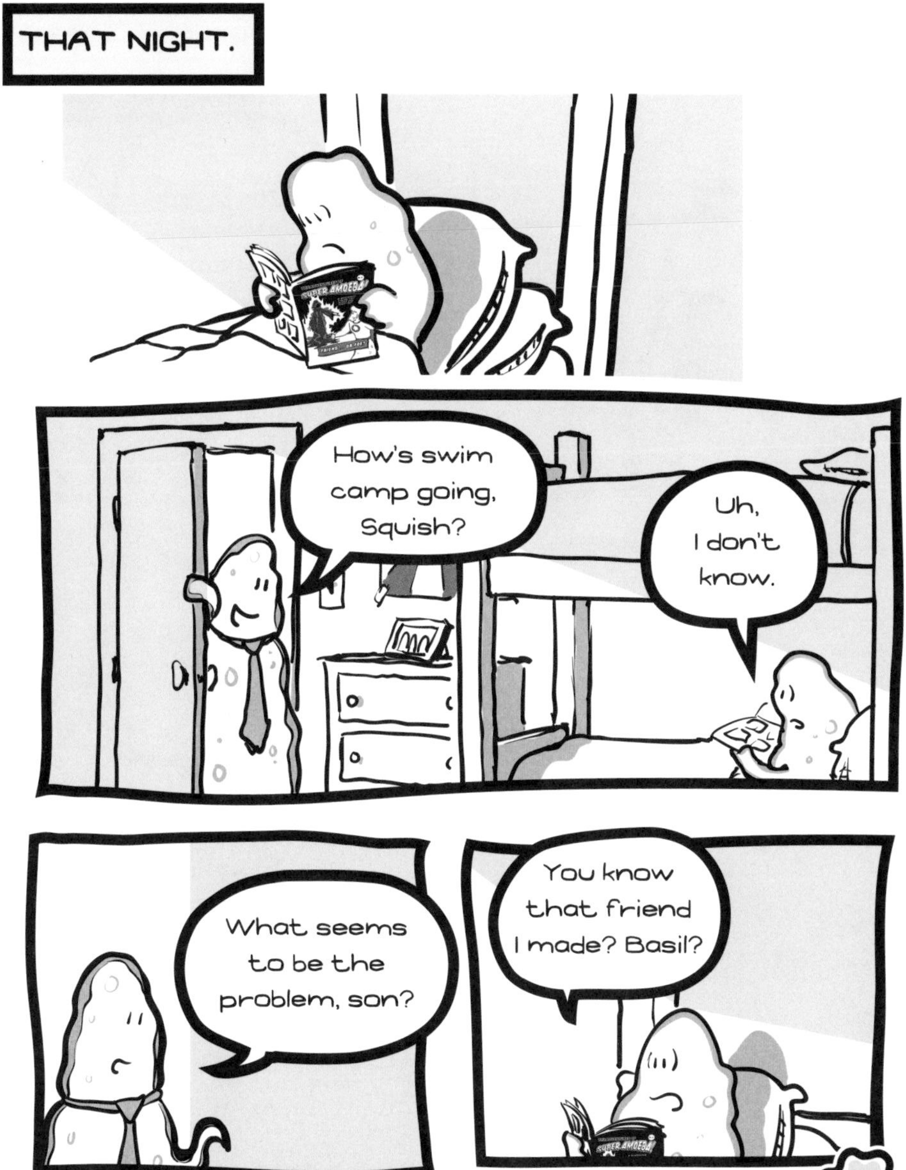
THAT NIGHT.
How's swim camp going, Squish?
Uh, I don't know.
What seems to be the problem, son?
You know that friend I made? Basil?

67

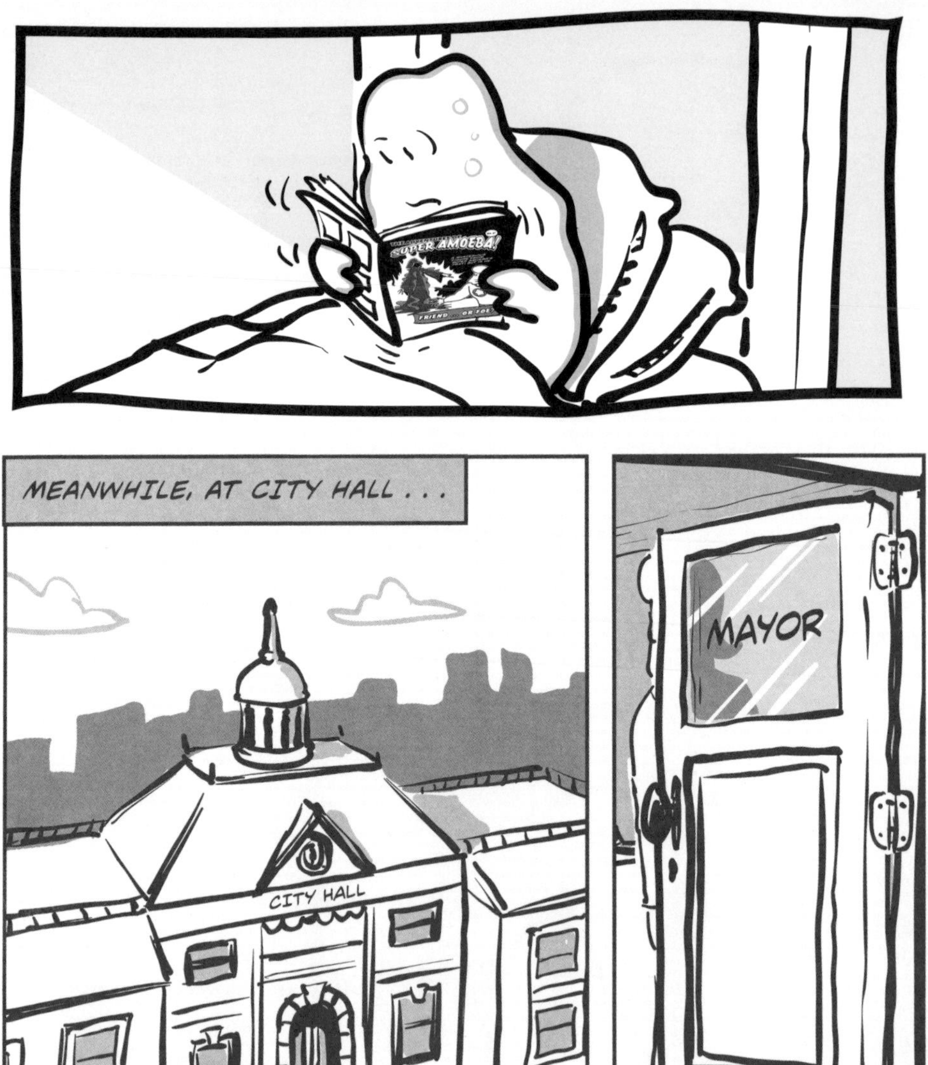
SUPER AMOEBA!
FRIEND ... OR FOE?
MEANWHILE, AT CITY HALL . . .
CITY HALL
MAYOR

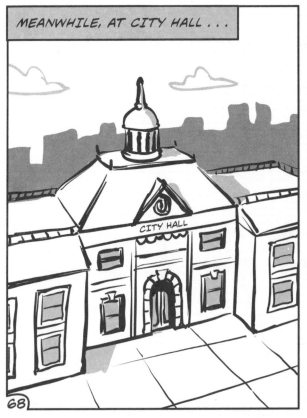

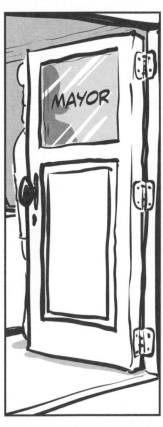

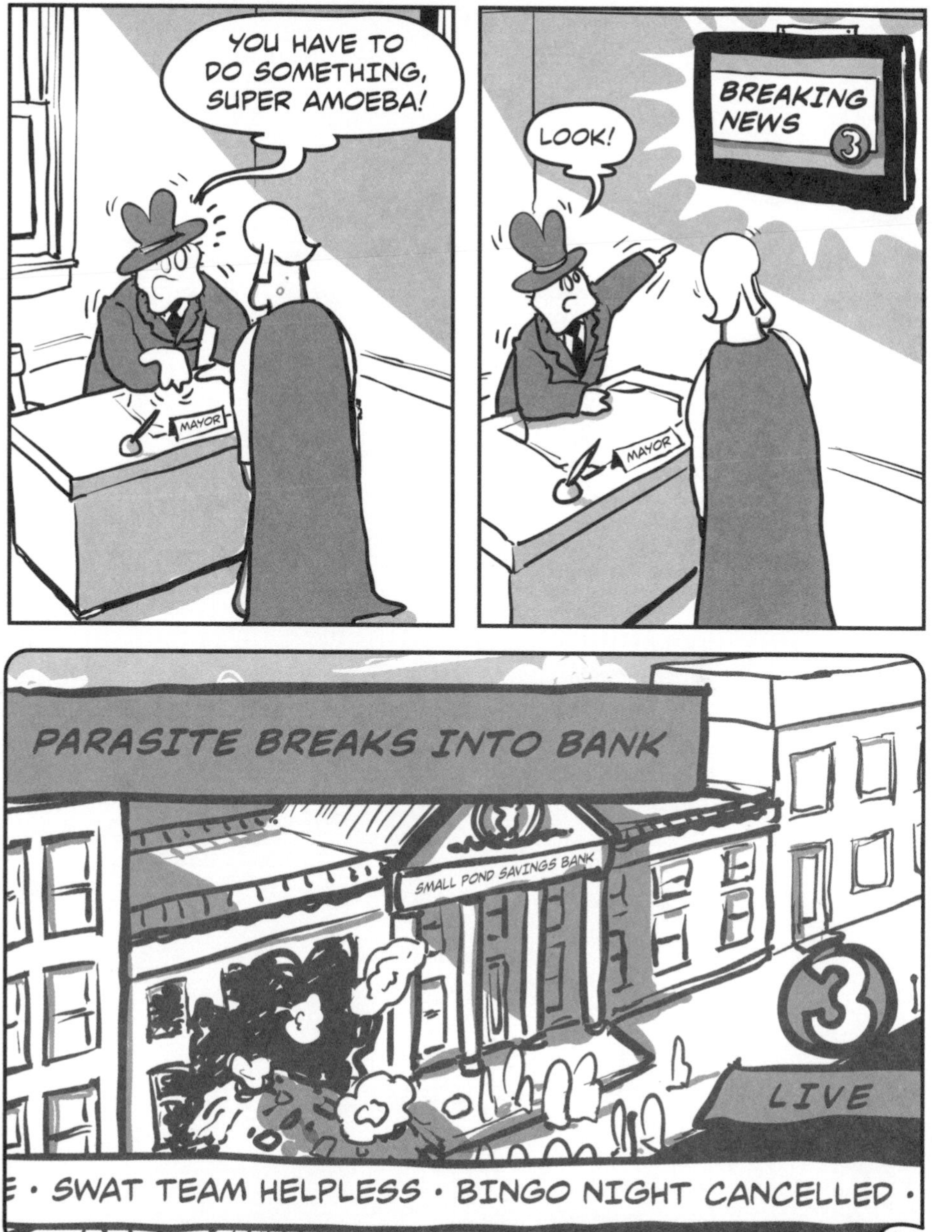
YOU HAVE TO DO SOMETHING, SUPER AMOEBA!
MAYOR
LOOK!
BREAKING NEWS
3
MAYOR
PARASITE BREAKS INTO BANK
SMALL POND SAVINGS BANK
3
LIVE
E • SWAT TEAM HELPLESS • BINGO NIGHT CANCELLED •

72

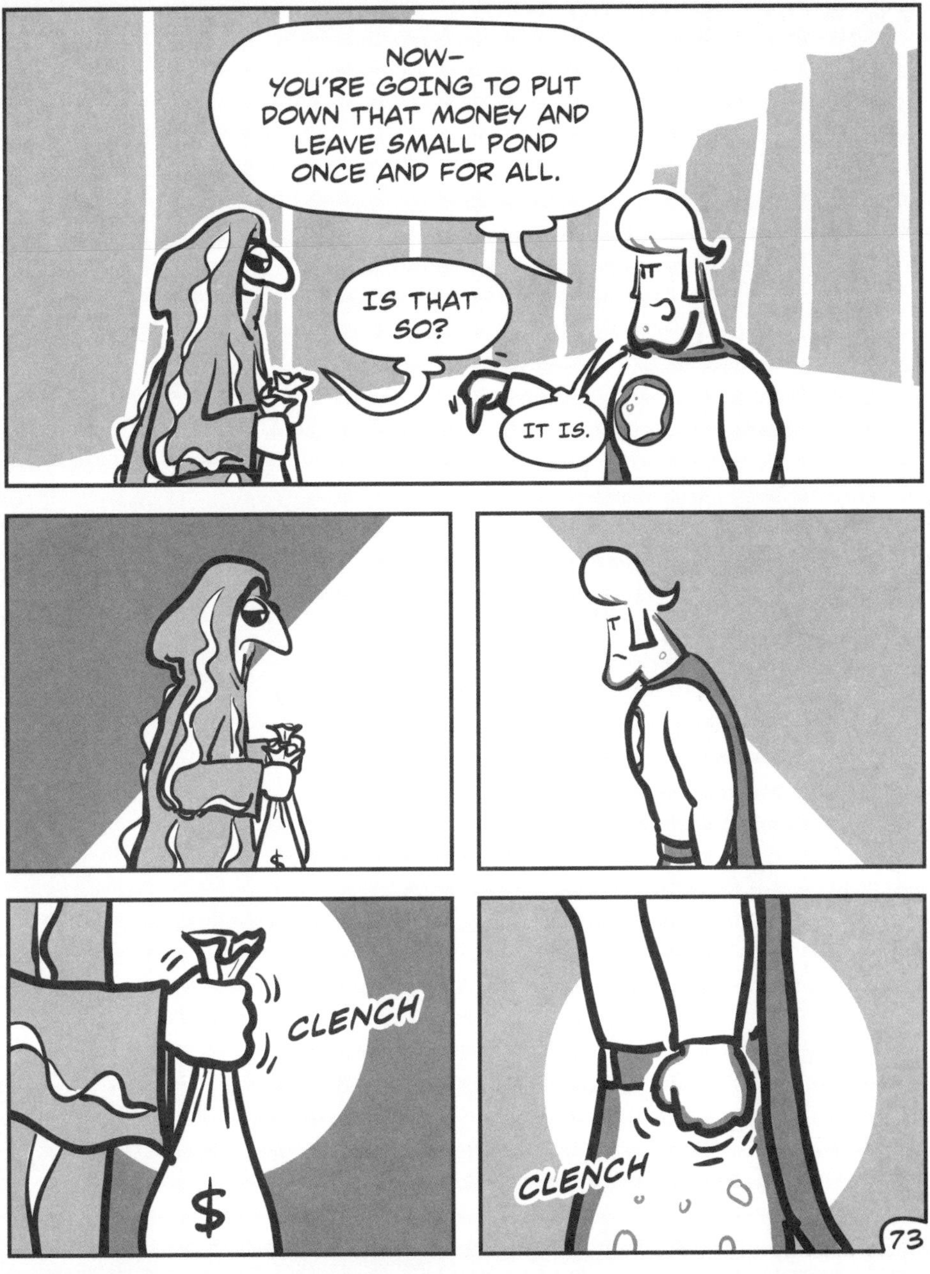
NOW–
YOU'RE GOING TO PUT DOWN THAT MONEY AND LEAVE SMALL POND ONCE AND FOR ALL.
IS THAT SO?
IT IS.
CLENCH
CLENCH

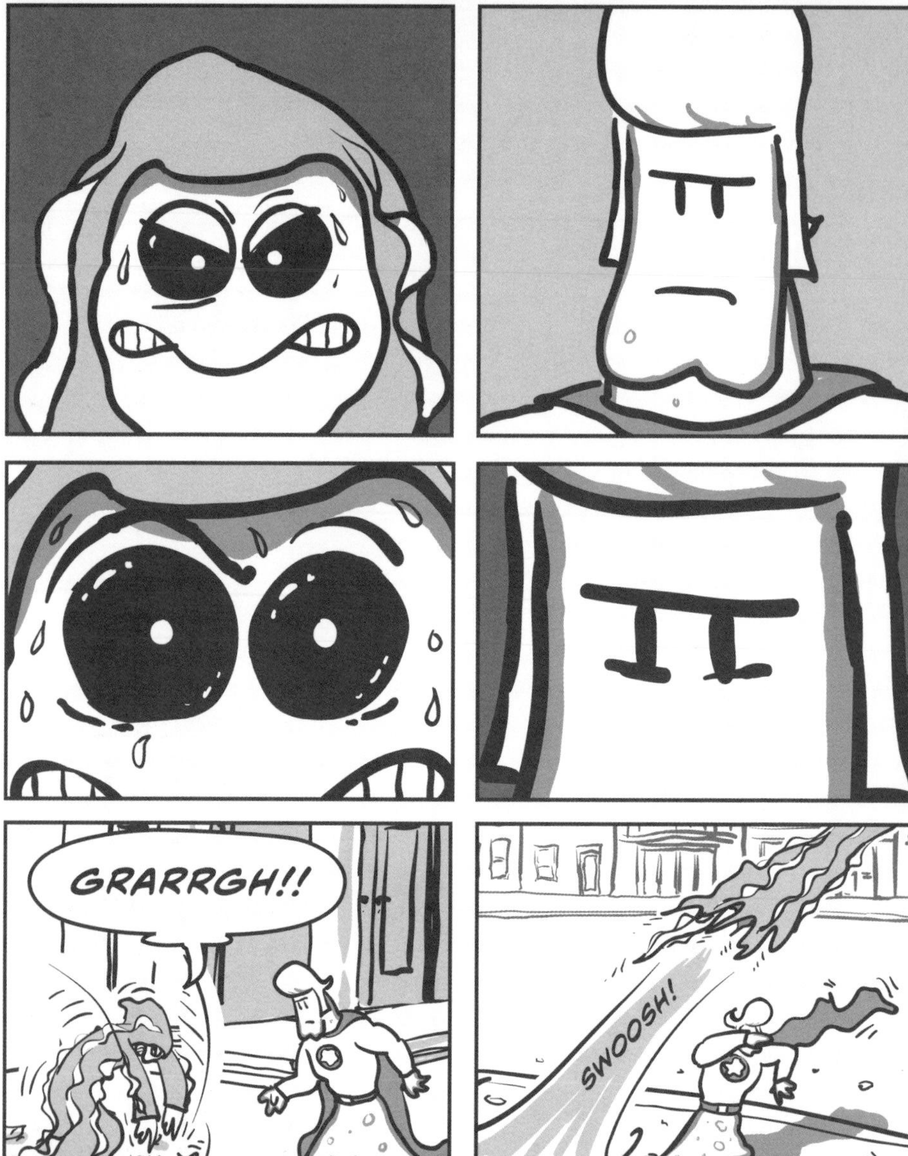
GRARRGH!!
THUNK!
WHUMP!
SWOOSH!

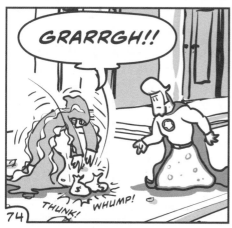

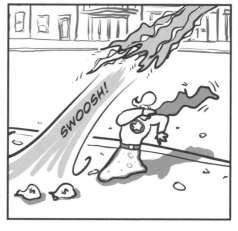

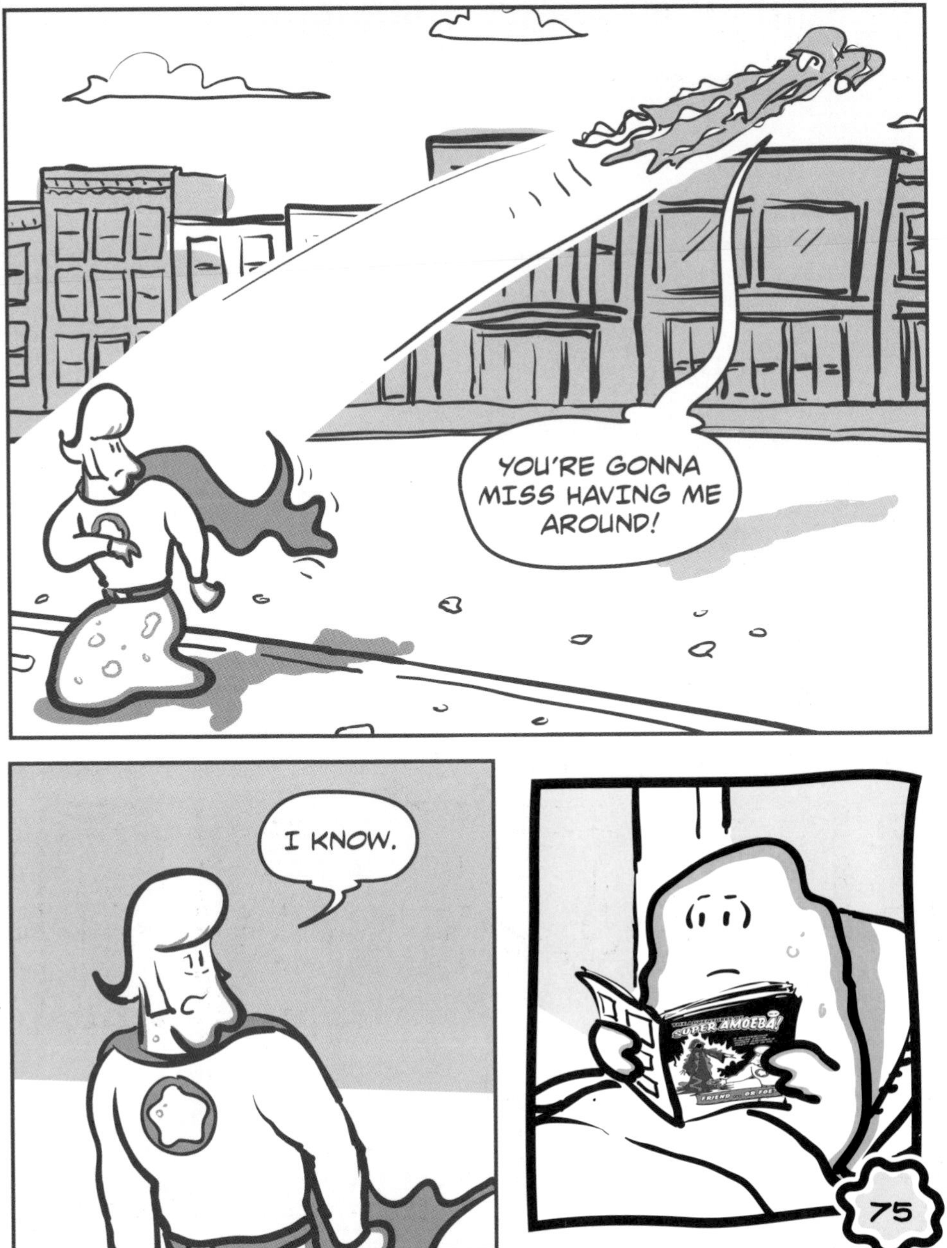
YOU'RE GONNA MISS HAVING ME AROUND!
I KNOW.
SUPER AMOEBA!

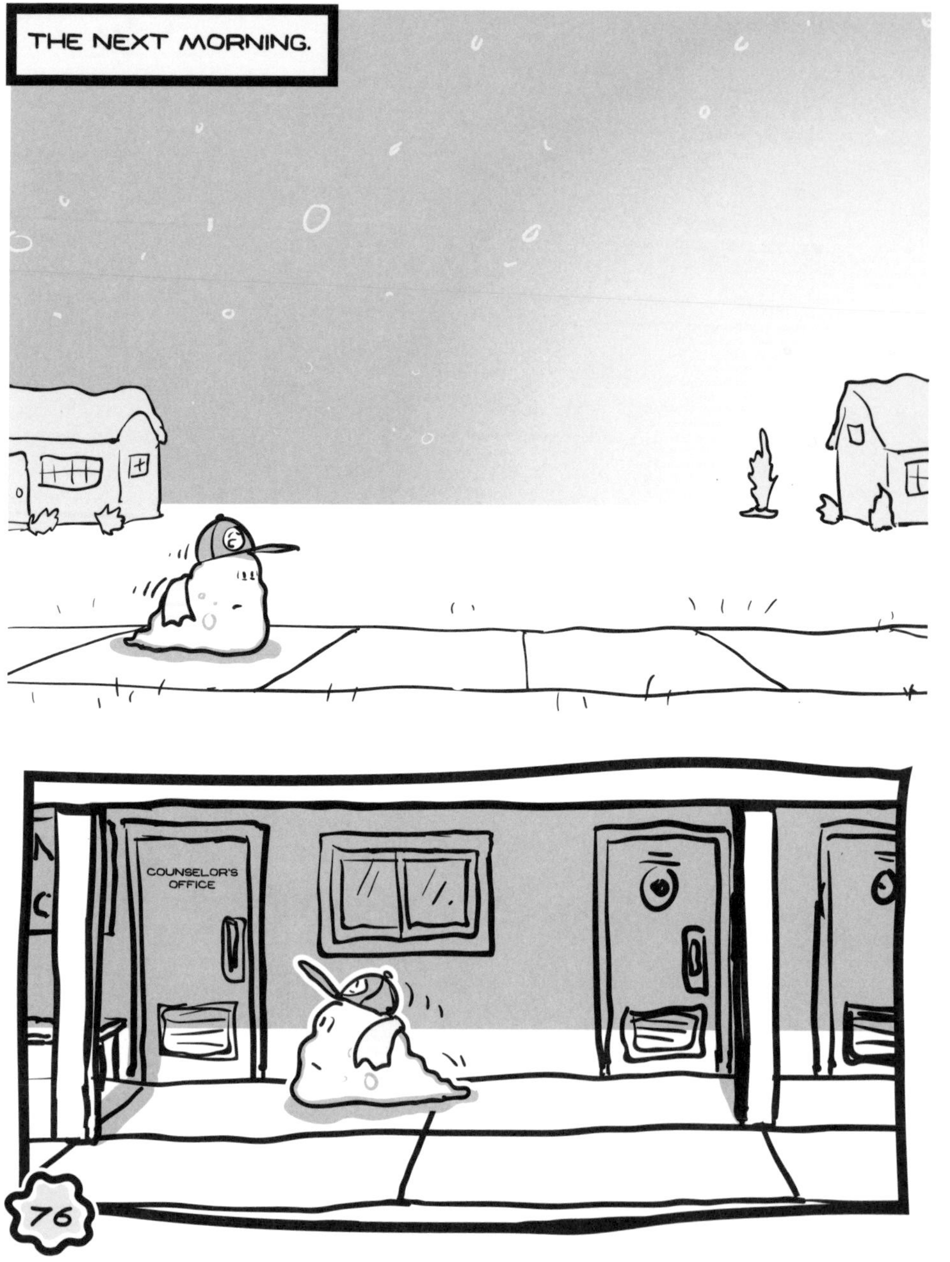
THE NEXT MORNING.
COUNSELOR'S OFFICE

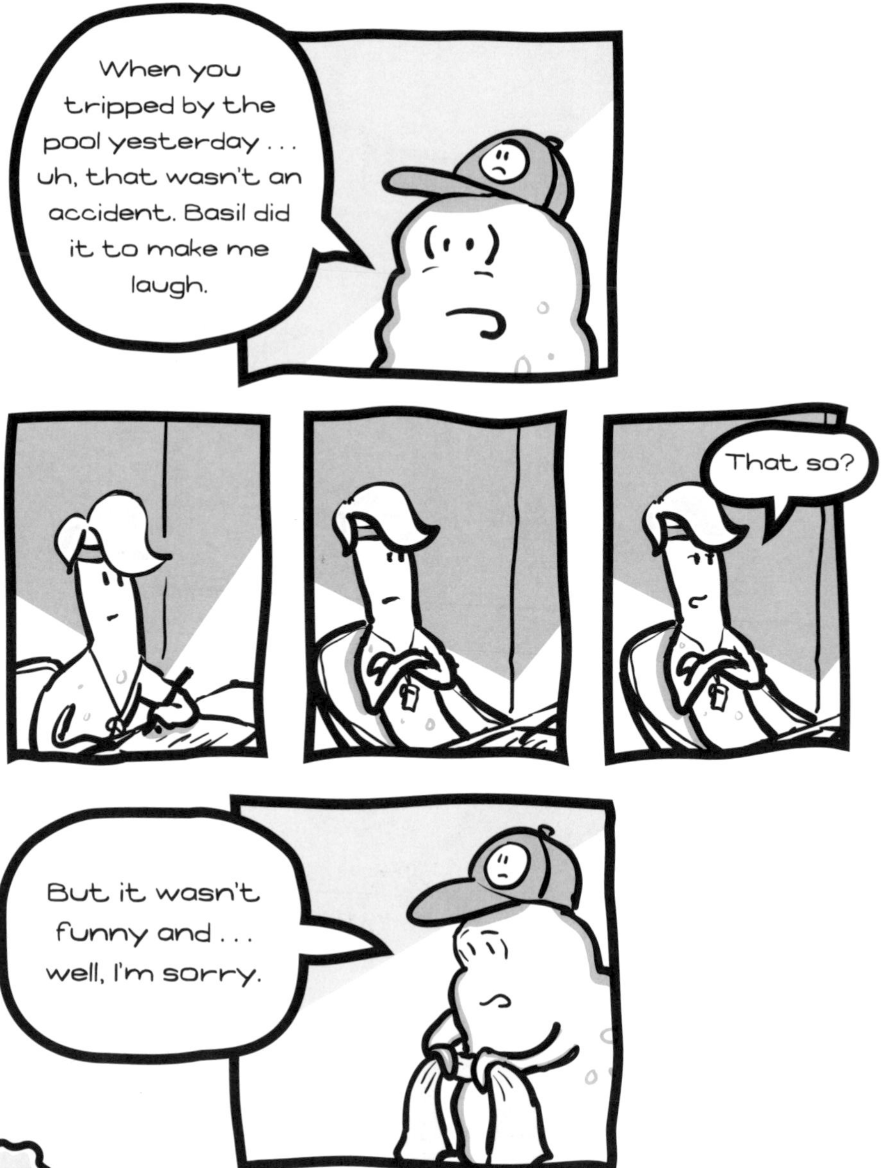
When you tripped by the pool yesterday . . . uh, that wasn't an accident. Basil did it to make me laugh.
That so?
But it wasn't funny and . . . well, I'm sorry.

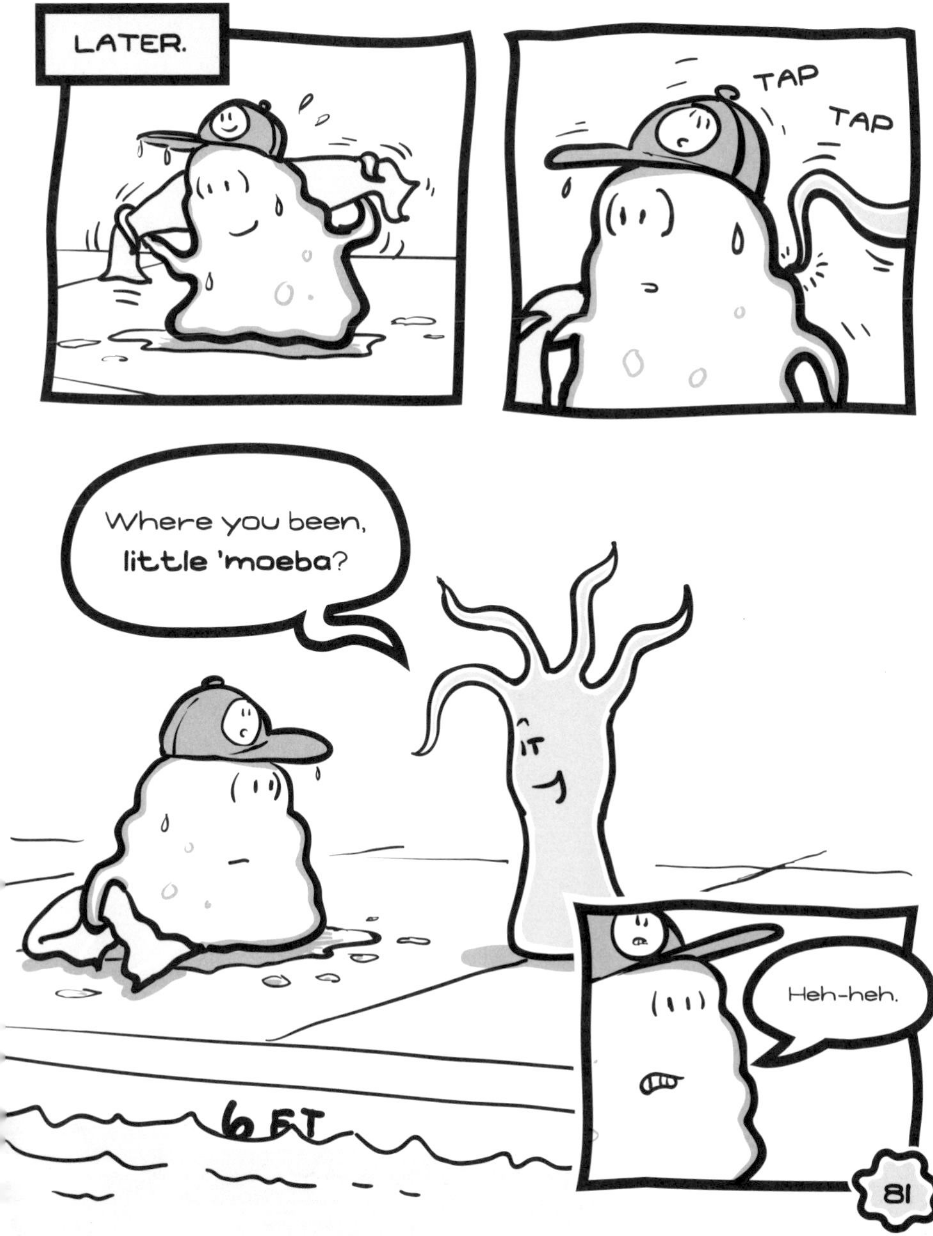
LATER.
TAP
TAP
Where you been, little 'moeba?
6 FT
Heh-heh.

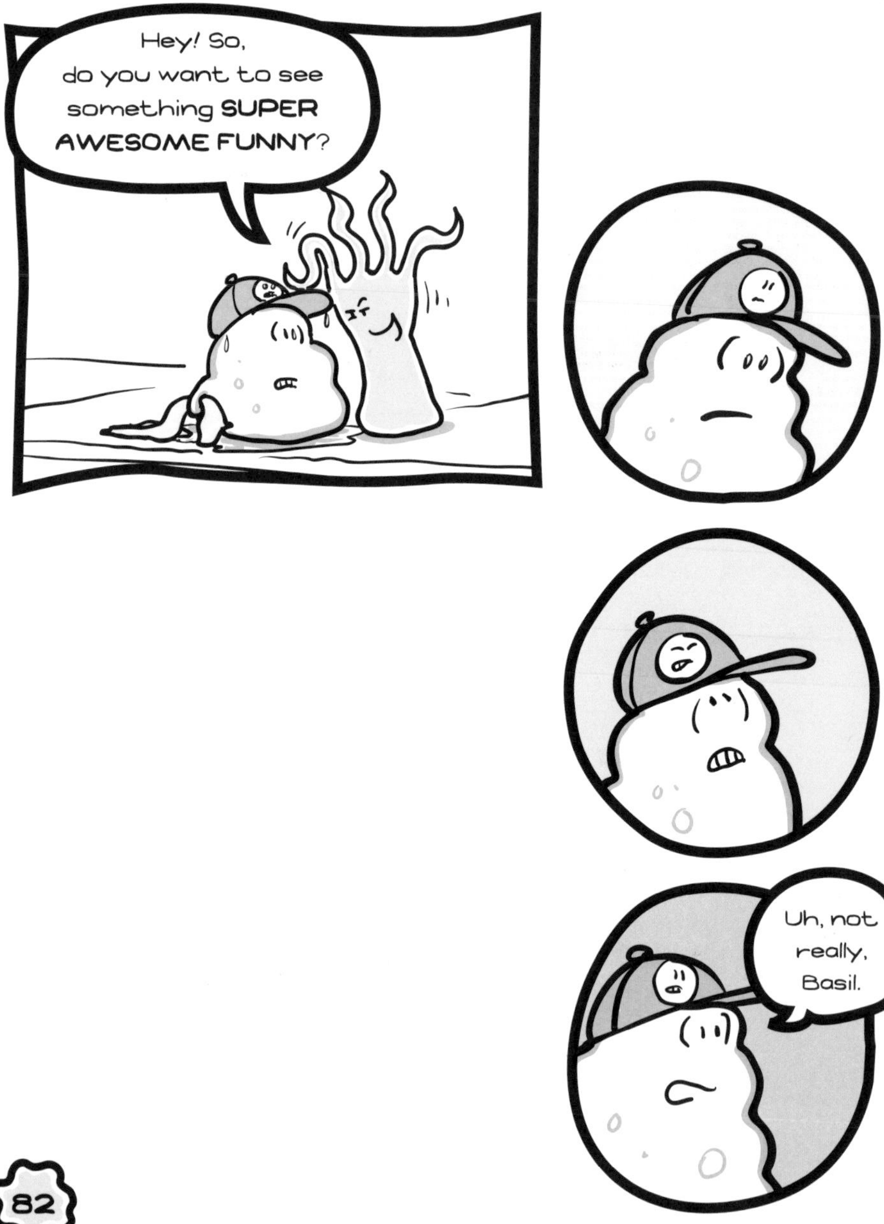
Hey! So, do you want to see something SUPER AWESOME FUNNY?
Uh, not really, Basil.

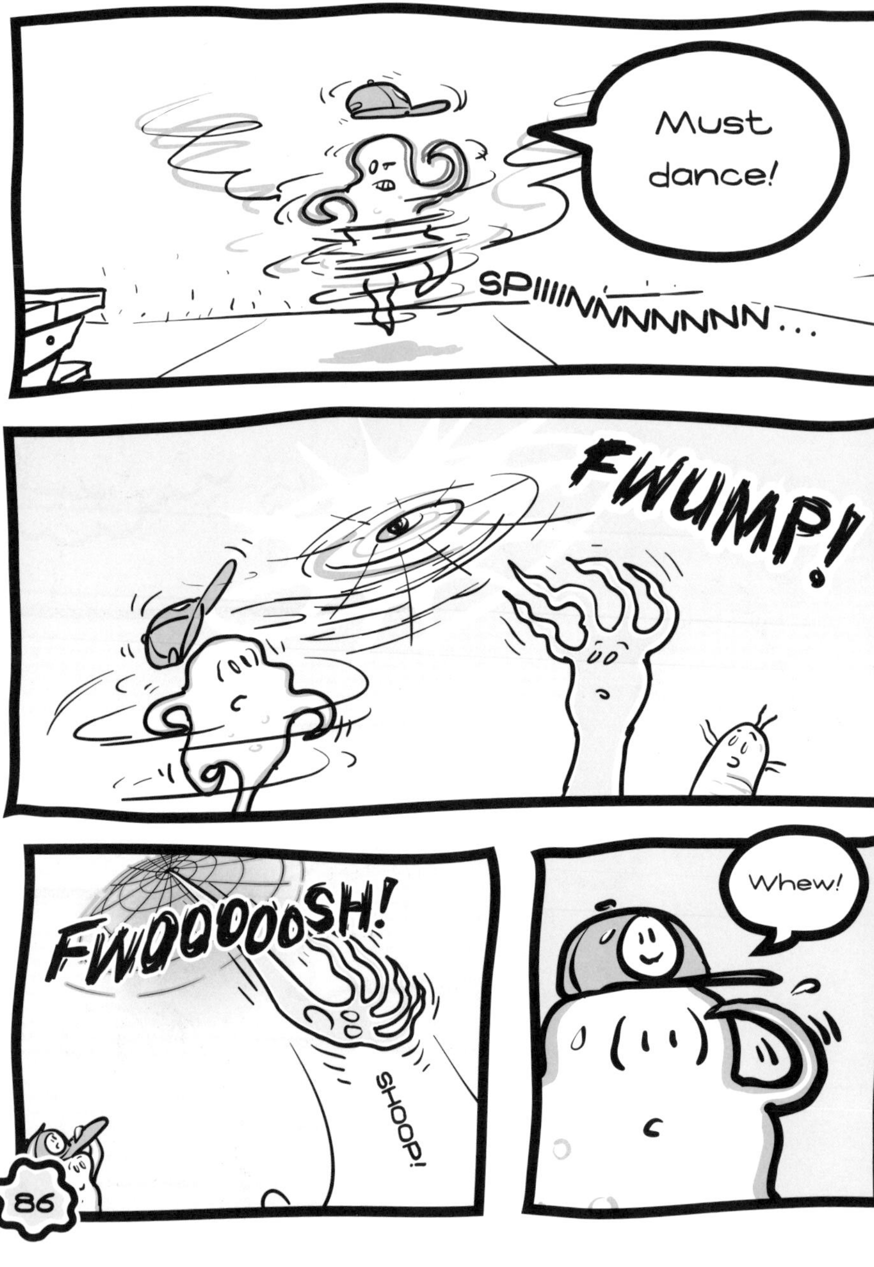

Must dance!
SPIIIINNNNNNNN...
FWUMP!
FWOOOOOOSH!
SHOOP!
Whew!

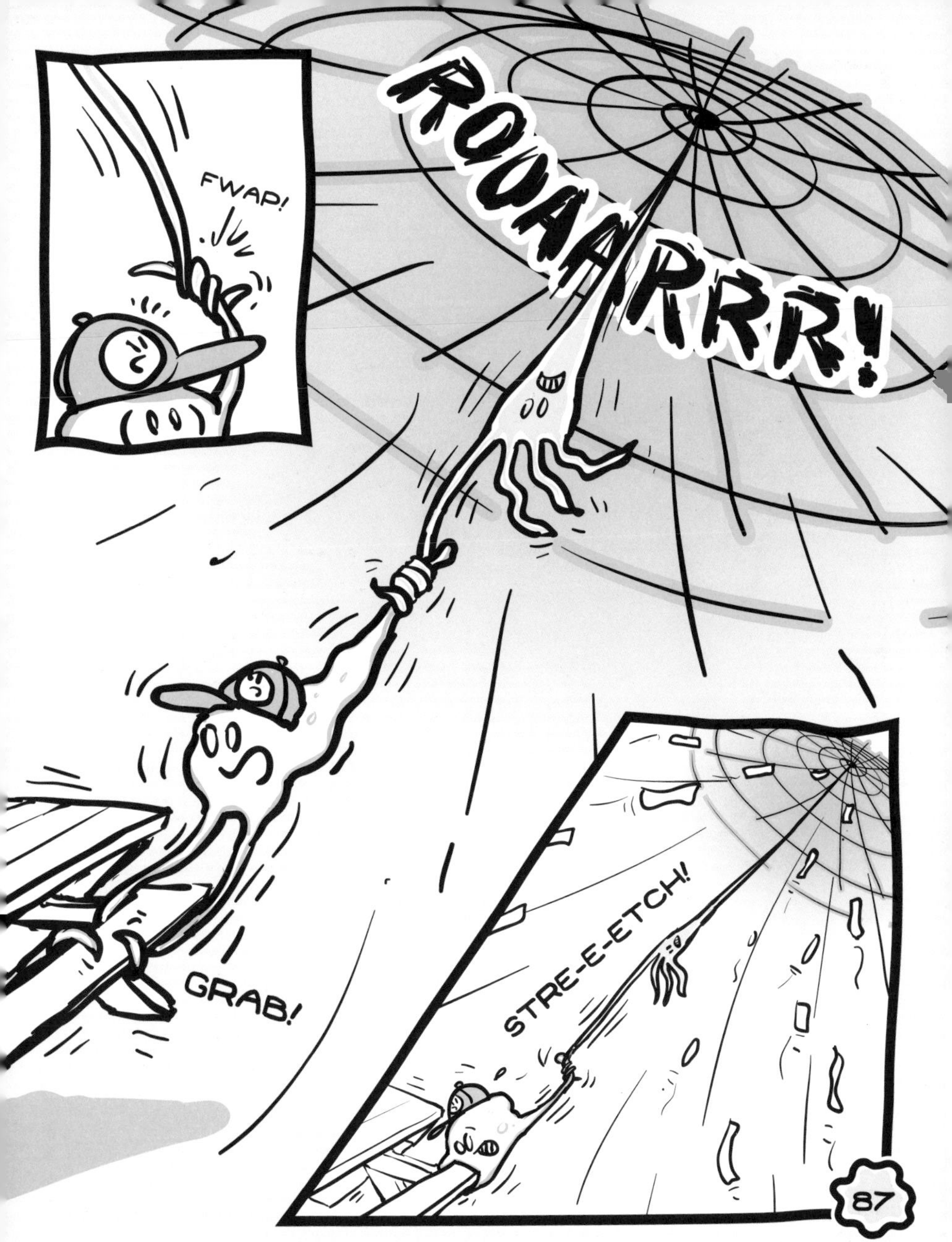
FWAP!
ROOAARRRR!
GRAB!
STRE-E-ETCH!

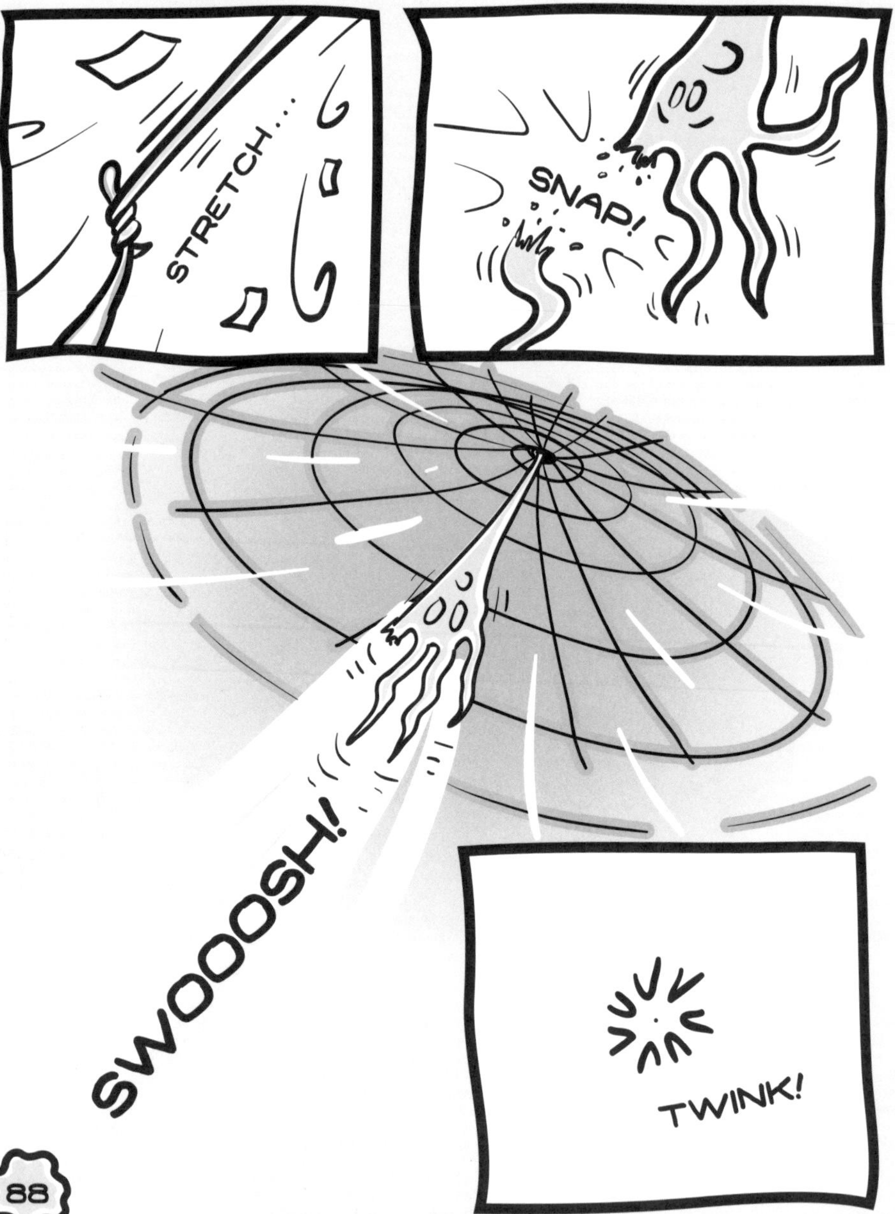
STRETCH...
SNAP!
SWOOOSH!
TWINK!

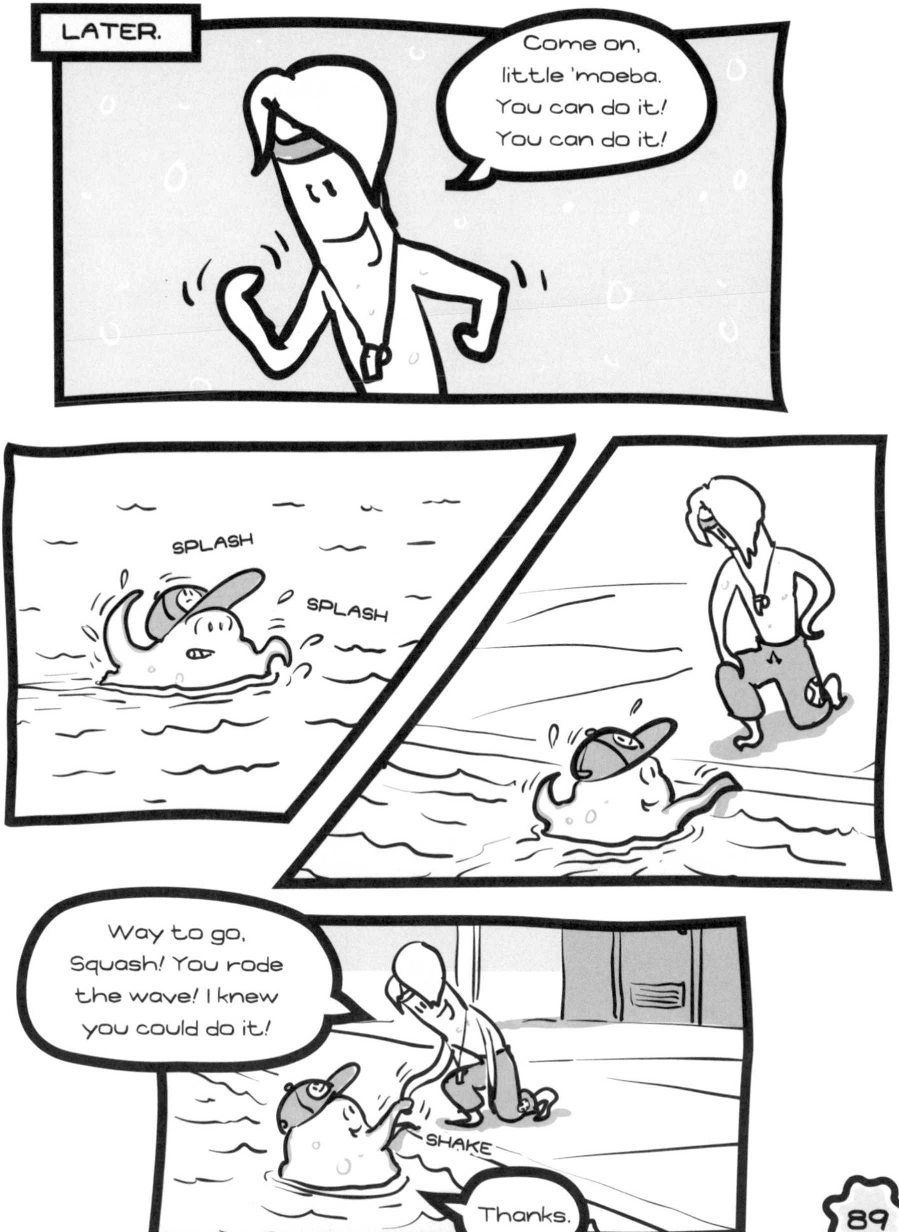
LATER.
Come on, little 'moeba. You can do it! You can do it!
SPLASH
SPLASH
Way to go, Squash! You rode the wave! I knew you could do it!
SHAKE
Thanks.

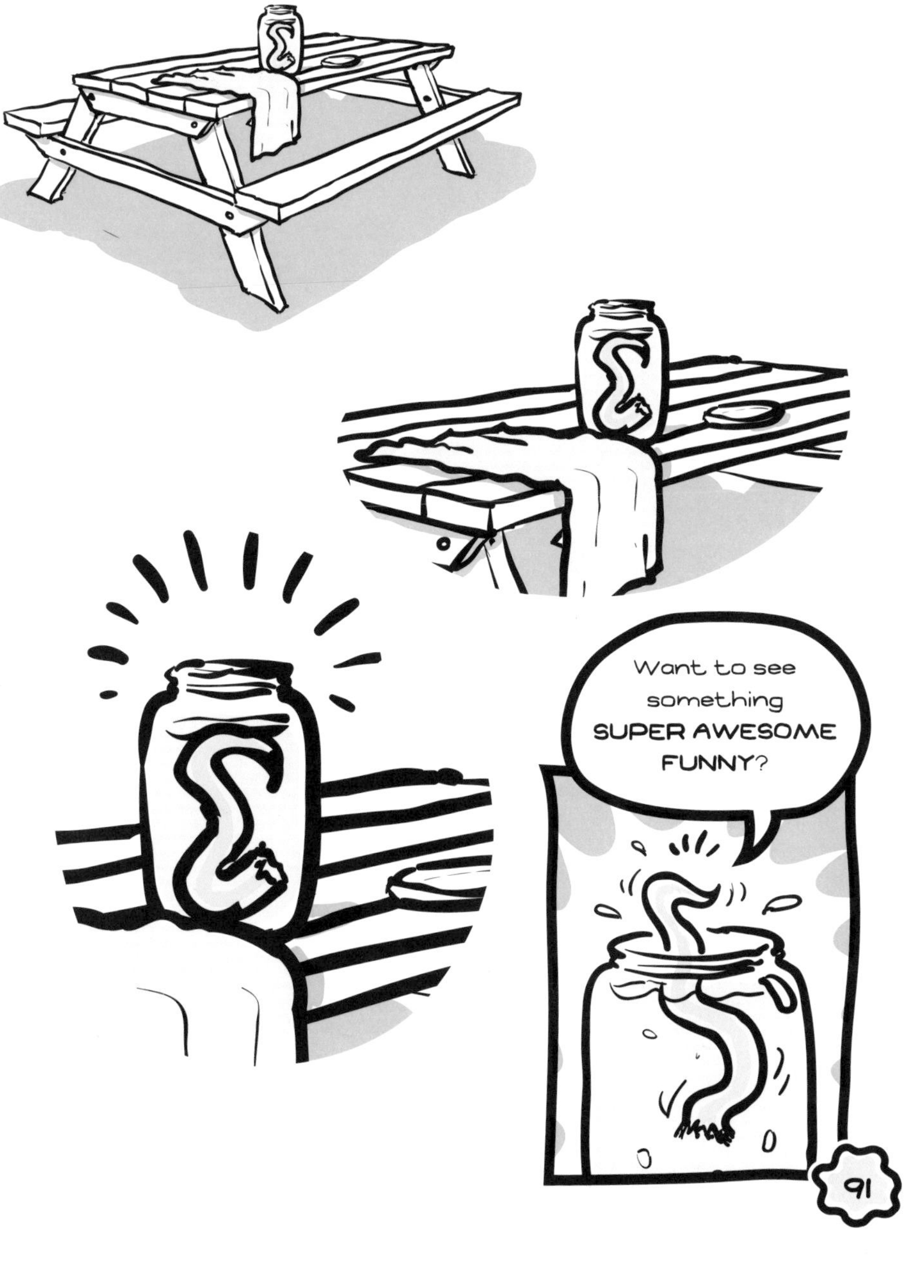
Want to see
something
SUPER AWESOME
FUNNY?

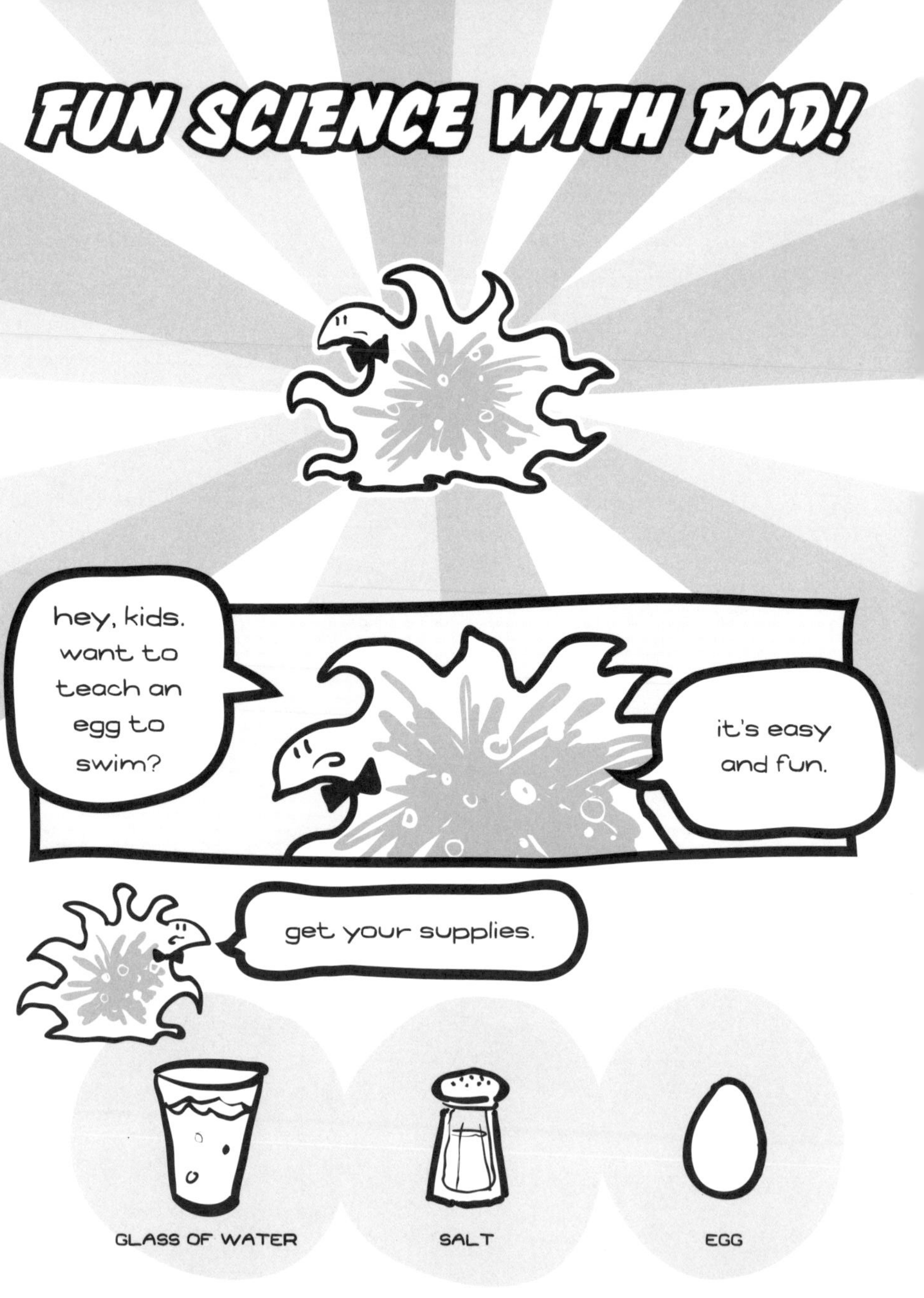
FUN SCIENCE WITH POD!
hey, kids. want to teach an egg to swim?
it's easy and fun.
get your supplies.
GLASS OF WATER
SALT
EGG

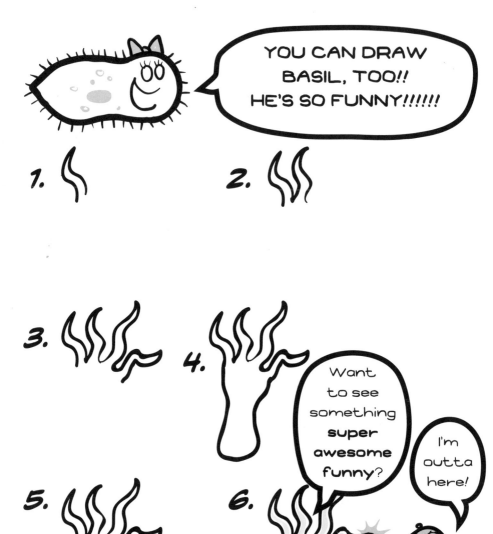